LUCKY CHARMER

PICK-UP LINES BOOK 2

KAYT MILLER

Sadie: The Palmer Sisters Book 3

Cortland: The Palmer Sisters Book 4

Keely: The Palmer Sisters Book 5

Violet: The Palmer Sisters Book 6

Molly: The Palmer Sisters Book 7

The Portrait Painter

Hopeful Romantic

Thanks to Margie Dill

DEDICATION

*To my eighty+ year-old mom who, after beta reading my first book,
said,
"You know... I think you need one more sex scene."
I love that woman!*

And to Becky Johnson. You are amazing.

COPYRIGHT

This book is a work of fiction. Names, characters, places, and incidents are the product of the author's imagination or are used facetiously. Any resemblance to actual events, locales, or persons, living or dead, is coincidental.

✽ Created with Vellum

CONTENTS

BECKLYN

"Whatʼre you doing here, Becklyn?"

Damn. *Busted.*

The voice is coming from my left side. A low rumble, right in my ear. I know who it is, too. His is a voice I know well. Heck, I dream about it. Sadly, I thought I was doing a good job avoiding him. Him and my brother.

"Uh…"

The voice—well, the man with the voice—is now in front of me, and the sight takes my breath away for just a second. That is, until he practically growls at me, "Go home."

My god, the man is surly. And totally hot at the same time. Honestly, I think I like him best when he's hot *and* surly.

"I'm just looking for a-a friend." No, I'm not.

Hot and surly crosses his arms over his chest, and that's when I know I'm going to have to do a whole lot better at convincing him. "What friend?" he asks with brow arched disbelievingly.

"Oh, you wouldn't know her."

"Try me, Becklyn."

Fark. When he says my name like *that*, chills run down my spine. In a good way.

"Her name is…" *Think fast. Think fast.* "Cameron Alderon."

"*Alderaan?*" He glares down at me. "Like the planet in *Star Wars?*"

And that—that right there—is why I. *Love.* This. Man. He's double-decker hot *and* he knows *Star Wars* trivia. But I can't let on that I feel that way about him. No. Way. I need to keep the farce going as long as I can. "No." I scoff loudly. "Geesh, you're such a nerd."

Lucky's face blushes. I think I may have hurt his feelings or something. He quickly rebounds and snaps, "I'm not a nerd."

"Nerd is the new jock, Lucky. Haven't you heard?"

"I ask again. *What* are you doing here?" He looks back toward the kitchen of the house he shares with three other guys. "Joe's gonna flip his shit if he sees you here."

Did I mention that one of his roommates is my oldest brother, Joe?

"Why would he care?" I mean, yes, he's going to care, because Joe is the oldest, I'm the youngest. He's always been *waaaaay* too protective of me, but now that I'm here, at the same college as him, he can't expect me to just stay home, especially on St. Patrick's Day. We're Irish, for gosh sakes. Plus, Joe has been bragging about his stupid St. Paddy's Day party *for years*. It's like the only party in the entire college town worth anything (according to my brother). And now that I'm a college student, I'm *not* missing this party. I wasn't lying when I said I was looking for a friend. In this case, it's my roommate. She came with me but ditched me at the door, which is fine since… hello… this is my brother's house.

Joe's claims of party lore were true. This place is p-a-c-k-e-d. And loud. I'm surprised I can even hear Lucky berating me, but his voice carries. That, and he's bent down so his face is in front of me, so even if I couldn't hear him, I could read his lips.

And boy, does Lucky have nice lips.

Gah! Why does he have to be so dang gorgeous?

Here's a better question… Why do I have to have a thing for him? Why can't I daydream and fantasize about the dorky guy in my biology lab? Huh? He's at least attainable. Sort of.

At that moment, a guy sidles up to me, wraps his arm around my shoulders, and drunkenly mumbles, "Hey, there, cutie. Why don't you be like St. Patrick and drive the snake out of my pants?"

I'm not sure if I should laugh or be affronted. Looking over at him, I can tell you that he's sort of cute. That is, if you're into guys who aren't into personal grooming. Don't get me wrong, I'm not desperate. I'm just tired of being single. Nineteen years of singledom sort of sucks. Heck, not even a prom date for this girl.

I sound pathetic.

Cue the encouraging monologue: *You don't need a man, Becklyn Morrissey. You're great just the way you are. If a guy can't see that, well, screw him.*

Wow, that's better. Inner Becklyn is right. Screw Lucky Ganetti.

"Marty. The fuck?"

This guy Marty acts like he didn't see Lucky standing right next to me. "What? Oh, hey, Lucky."

"What the hell? That's Joe's little sister, Marty." Lucky scowls. "You're trying to pick up Joe's little sister. He's gonna kick your ass."

That's when things take a bad turn. Marty, now not as cute, says, "Little?" He looks me up and down and points. "He's got a bigger one than *that*?"

And now it's my turn to blush. Because Marty just hit on something that has caused me a lot of hurt over the years. My weight.

You don't need a man, Becklyn Morrissey. You're great just the way you are. If a guy can't see that, well, screw him.

I know I'm overweight. Of course I do. It's not something that people just ignore, sadly. But for some reason, people think it's okay to talk to you about it. Like, take the grocery store. I don't know how many times I've had people, mostly women, thin women, feel like it's a teachable moment when they see cheese doodles in my cart. They say stuff like, "You know, honey, you'd be gorgeous if you'd lay off the processed foods."

It's true. I should lay off processed foods, but those items are cheaper and, if I'm being honest, they're delicious.

And it's not like I haven't tried losing weight. I've started Weightloss Wishers multiple times; I've tried the paleo diet and the low carb diet. Sure, they work, at first. Then, they don't. I'm to blame, of course. If I could stick with them, I'm sure I'd be fit and fabulous by now, but I end up going off whatever fad diet it is, and I gain the weight, plus some, back.

Plus, it's not like I don't exercise. I like walking and riding my bike occasionally. Then there's the fact my roommate and I enjoy dancing around our dorm room. Plus, I eat okay, which isn't easy when all anyone *ever* wants to do in the dorm is order pizza. Have I gained the freshman fifteen since I got here last semester? Guilty as charged. But I'm working on it.

What? *I am.*

More importantly, I'm also working on accepting myself the way I am. I mean, I'm fighting heredity here, and believe me when I say it's a thing.

My mind stops wandering when I hear Lucky growl at Marty, "The fuck you say?"

Marty holds up his hands like he's getting robbed at gunpoint. "Sorry, man." He sounds a little scared. I don't blame him, because people don't mess with Lucian "Lucky" Ganetti.

Rumor has it his family has ties to the mafia underworld.

The rumors are wrong. His dad is a plumber, and his mom was a kindergarten teacher. His mom, Molly, whom I never got to meet, died in some kind of accident when he was five. The worst possible age to lose your mom—not that any age is good.

The rumors, while untrue, have given him a reputation as someone to fear. Joe says he likes that because people leave him alone, for the most part. Plus, there's the fact Lucky is a big guy. I'm talking b-i-g. And not fat, like me. He's buff because his hobby is boxing. He loves it. I've never seen him do it, but according to Joe, "Lucky is the bomb in the ring." I don't get it, personally. Bouncing around a square, punching each other does not sound the least bit fun.

I believe Joe when he says Lucky is a good boxer, though. Joe doesn't make up stuff. Especially about Lucky.

"I didn't know she was your girl, man." Marty is digging himself deeper into a hole.

"You just fucking told Joe's baby sister you wanted her to fuck you. He's going to lose his goddamn mind. You might as well leave now and never step foot in here again, you utter fucking tool."

Ooh, wow. I don't think I've ever heard Lucky say that many words in a row. He's more of a five- or six-word sentence guy. And that's when he's feeling especially chatty. I know this to be true because I've known him practically my whole life. Well, half my life. He moved to our hometown when I was eleven. Even then, I knew that there was something special about him. He wasn't all muscley back then, but he had that longish, wavy dark hair and those caramel-colored eyes. He still has both of those things, although his hair is way shorter now. It still looks good. Everything about Lucky is good.

"Go home, Becklyn."

Okay. I take it back. Not everything is good. This side of him sure isn't.

"Come on, Lucky. I'm a college student now. It's a rule that I get to go to college parties."

He points at the red cup in my hand. "What are you drinking?"

I glance down at my hand and back up at him. "Water."

"It's green."

"Green water." I shrug. "It's St. Patty's day."

Lucky moves an inch or two closer, bending until I swear I can smell him.

He smells really good.

"Blow on me."

Oh, wow. I know he wants to smell my breath, but if you remove one of those words, the middle one, well, that's funny. I snicker. I can't help it. It's what I do.

"Becklyn Marie…"

I stop laughing. The laughter is replaced with a scowl, because I'm instantly angry. "Do *not* use my middle name like you're my father." He's not my father. He's the man I'm going to marry, and if I'm going to accomplish that feat, he's going to have to stop thinking of me as some little kid.

I'm not a kid.

I'm a *woman*. With boobs now, and everything.

Sure, it took a while, but they're there, and I'm not going to lie, they're impressive. I prove it by pushing my chest out just enough to bump into the arms he's still got crossed over his chest like he's about to ground me or something.

He must notice, because he immediately pushes himself up to his full height, looks down at my chest, and steps back. "You…" He glances around the room as a blush hits his high cheekbones. "You just need to go."

"No." I shake my head. "I'm here for the 'famous'"—I use air quotes—"St. Patrick's Day party." I hold up my glass. "And I'm having some green beer." I glare at him. "Deal with it."

Taking a step to my right, his left, I'm about to make my escape when I feel his hand on my upper arm. Then, his breath is on my cheek. "I'm watching you."

I'm suddenly breathless. In a good way. I find bravery—from where, I'm not sure. Turning my head until we're looking eye to eye, I do something I'm going to tell my grandchildren someday. The grandchildren I'm going to have thanks to the children I'm going to have with Lucky Ganetti. I lean in slowly. You know, to give him time to process. When he doesn't move, I press my lips to his for just a second. Long enough for two things to happen. One, to make my point, and two, so I get a chance to feel just how soft his lips really are.

They're soft.

Very soft.

I say, "You do what you need to do, Lucky. Go ahead and watch me have some fun." I pull away from him, and his hand slips from my arm. With my back to him, I smile, because at that moment, I feel pretty dang kick-ass.

2

BECKLYN

"DID YOU JUST KISS THAT GUY?" MY ROOMMATE, DEENA, ASKS. There's pride in her voice. Something I haven't heard from her— at least as it relates to me.

"I did."

"Why?"

"Did you see him? Why wouldn't I kiss him?" Okay, that's false bravado. I quickly tell her the story. "I know him. He grew up down the street, and he's my brother's best friend."

"Are you two a thing?" She looks shocked. I suppose I don't blame her. If I saw someone like me kissing someone like him, I'd have questions. "Because, if so, you've been holding back on me. Are you two hooking up after?" She reaches up with both hands and starts to play with her long, pretty blonde curls. She does that when she's thinking. "I get it. That's why you insisted on coming to this party."

"I told you. This party is *legendary.*"

She looks around the place, shrugs, and says, "I've been to better." Still twirling her hair around her fingers, she starts tapping her foot.

Foot tapping. That's a sign she has an idea.

9

"You should totally go for that guy. He hasn't stopped looking over here since you kissed him."

I'm so tempted to look back over my shoulder, but I resist. "Nah." I shake my head. "He's only doing that to make sure I don't do anything stupid."

"Nuh-uh." She shakes her head. "*I* know guys…"

She does. Lots and lots of guys.

"And that one"—she nods in his direction which freaks me out a bit because he'll know we're talking about him—"is into you."

I scoff. "No." *I wish.*

"Okay." She places one hand on my shoulder. "Let's test my hypotenuse."

"You mean, hypothesis?"

"Whatever." She rolls her big blue eyes. "We'll find you a guy to flirt with." She leans forward. "A really drunk one." She winks.

I'm not sure what that means. Why does he have to be drunk?

"We'll let the guy kind of grope you a little and see what Thor does about it."

"Thor is blond."

"Whatever." Deena scans the room, back and forth, and stops. "Got him." She uses her arm to turn me until I'm facing the living room. "See that guy on the sofa?"

I locate the sofa and spot her target. He's slumped over a bit, a red cup in his hand that is slowly dripping green beer onto the carpet. I don't know about Deena's plan, but the least I can do is save Joe's carpeting from a green stain. I look down at the floor and realize it's too late.

"Go on." She pushes my shoulder. "Go talk to him."

I don't want to. Besides, I think the guy is asleep. Why wake him? "Can't we just wait and see if someone comes to us?" I mean, Marty did try to hit on me. Yes, that ended badly but still…

"Go." She pushes me again. "Let's see what the brown-haired Thor does."

"Brown-haired Thor?" God, she really needs more variety in her television viewing. Something other than just *The Real Housewives*.

"Fine." Stomping over to the couch, I reach down and take the cup from the drunk guy. As I set it on the table next to the sofa, he suddenly wakes up.

"Hey," he says with a scowl. "The fuck you doing?"

Oh, wow. He's angry.

As he pushes himself up, I realize he's quite tall. Like collegiate basketball player tall. He's also very unsteady.

"You took my beer, you bitch," he spits, but fortunately, since he's up a couple stories, that spittle misses me.

"I was just trying…"

That's when I realize tall guy is *really* drunk. His body starts to tilt left, then right. I'm talking a dramatic shifting. When it changes to back to front, I know I'm in trouble. And that's when all hell breaks loose because tall guy can't recover from the forward tilt. And sadly, I'm standing in front of him—

"Uh…" is all I'm able to get out of my mouth when he reaches out, placing his hands on my shoulders like I'm somehow going to be able to keep him upright. Physics makes that impossible. He's a foot taller than me. At least. He's moving in a downward trajectory. There's no hope. I do the only thing I can: I toss my cup aside and go down with the ship.

Hard.

Very hard.

Not only that, I go down at an awkward angle. My arm is behind my back, and my foot is turned sideways.

How did that happen?

This giant of a man is literally on top of me. And, unless I'm completely crazy, I think he's snoring.

"Help." I squeak because the weight of him on top of me is forcing the breath out of me.

"Becklyn." It's a man's voice.

Please don't be Joe. Because if he sees this, he'll kill this drunk guy first, then me.

I'm able to see who it is, because my face is between the guy's head and his shoulder. "Lucky?" I'm seriously having trouble breathing. "Help?" It comes out as a raspy squeak.

"Fuck." He sounds quite growly. With hardly any effort, he pushes the tall guy off my upper body. His long legs are still on top of mine. That is, until Lucky lifts up the guy's size-fifteen feet and flops them down onto the sofa. I look over at the man and see he's on his back now, still sawing logs.

"You okay?" Lucky's squatting down beside me now. "Can you get up?" His hands are hovering over me like he can't figure out if he should touch me and if so, where.

Rolling a little to my left, I'm able to get my right arm out from beneath my back. It hurts, but nothing like my ankle.

"My ankle." I wince as I attempt to move my foot.

"He stepped on your foot as you were going down." That comment is from Deena, who's standing over me, twirling her hair around with both hands and biting her bottom lip. That's her tell that she's nervous. "That's gonna leave a mark."

I don't know why, but her words make me crack the heck up. I mean, I need to laugh at this or else I'll cry. Especially since the party has essentially stopped and everyone, and I mean *everyone*, is now standing around me in a giant circle, staring.

"What the fuck, Becks?" And there he is. My brother, Joe. "What the fuck are you doing here?"

Ignoring him, I lift my arm out for Deena to help me up, but I get Lucky instead. "Come on. Let me help you up." I take his hand in mine, and I feel those tingles like they talk about in my favorite books. It's happened anytime I've accidentally touched Lucky.

He pulls on me until I'm sitting up. He slides his hand around my back and pulls us both up to our feet. The pain hits me like a ton of bricks.

"Down," I whine. "Let me sit down."

"No." Lucky growls. That's when he does the impossible. He slides his other arm beneath my knees and lifts.

To say it's embarrassing is an understatement because I hear several mutterings from the peanut gallery. Things like "Whoa, that dude is *strong*" and "He's gonna throw out his back."

Ignoring the comments, Lucky's focus is on me. "Time to go home, Becklyn."

"Put me down," I snap.

"I'll put you down in the car." He looks over at Deena. "You drive here?"

"Nope." She shakes her head while still messing with her stupid hair. "Walked."

"Joe." He looks to his left. "Grab my keys."

I try another route, because this is beyond embarrassing now. "You shouldn't drive. You've been drinking."

"No. I haven't." Lucky isn't looking at me. I guess he's got to pay attention to where he's walking. I turn and see he's making his way to the front door.

"I can walk." I really can't, but him carrying me is humiliating. For him.

"I've got you."

"I'm too heavy." I am.

"You're fine." He looks down at me quickly. I swear I glimpse a tiny smile. "You stink, though."

No wonder; I'm also wet. My back is, anyway, thanks to all the green beer that saturated the carpet and is now soaking my top and jeans.

"I bet," I grumble. "You guys need to get a Rug Doctor in there."

He snorts. "Probably right."

Probably right?

"YOU NEED TO ICE THAT ANKLE." LUCKY HAS JUST SET ME ON MY bed. He drove us back to the dorm, carried me to the elevator that took us up to the fifth floor, down the hall, and into our room. After Deena unlocked the door, he stepped into the tiny box of a room and asked, "Which one is yours?" I point to the bed with the baby blue comforter and way too many pillows.

Our room is really cute. Sure, it's tiny, but we've done our best to set it up the most efficient way. Deena's bed is lofted so there's room for a sofa beneath it. My bed sits atop our dressers, so the rest of the space is used for our desks and our dance parties.

"You got any ice?"

I shake my head. We've only got a tiny dorm refrigerator in our room, and it's one that doesn't have a freezer. Those were a lot more expensive.

"Shit," he mutters.

"I'm fine," I say, scooting back a little. "I'll just elevate it."

He looks at Deena. "Can you run and get her some ice from food service?"

She looks at the clock. "It's after nine. It's closed."

"Shit." He steps closer to me, reaches out, and gently touches my ankle. "You need ice."

"Go back to your party, Lucky. I'm fine."

"You sure?" His pretty face is all scrunched up. The man looks sincerely concerned, and I'm not going to lie, it makes me feel all warm inside.

"Positive." That's a lie. I need ice. My ankle has ballooned, and the color has already changed to a grotesque blueish-purple hue. Heck, I'm not sure it isn't broken.

"Yeah." He nods. "Okay." Turning, he reaches for the doorknob, because that's just how small our room is. "I'm sure Joe will check on you tomorrow."

No, he won't. He's pissed at me, which in Joe-land means he'll give me the silent treatment for a while.

A long while.

"Yep. I'm sure he will." I smile, hoping he'll leave. "Go have fun." I wave him off. I need for him to go. I need to cry because, no joke, my ankle *hurts*. "Thanks for bringing me home, Lucky."

"Okay." He nods. "Yeah. Bye."

And poof. He's gone.

The second the door clicks shut; Deena starts to cackle. "Oh. Em. Gee. *You're* a fucking genius."

"Huh?" I look over at her.

"That guy," she points at the door, "is totally in love with you. Your idea to let that guy fall on you was pure, goddamn genius."

"*Let him…* fall on me? I didn't—"

"And you got *him* to carry you?" Now she's practically beaming. "Not gonna lie, girl. *That* dude is strong." With a wink, she adds, "It just proves my point. He's in love with you."

"Uh." I practically scoff. "He's not."

"He is."

"No. He's not."

"He is." She stands, reaching for her towel. Sliding into her shower flip-flops, she says, "I'm gonna take a shower." Sadly, we don't have a private bath. We have to share a bathroom with everyone on this floor. As she steps over the threshold into the hall, she turns. "You know, I'm not the smartest person…"

That's an understatement, but what she lacks in book smarts, she makes up for in other ways.

"…but I'm never wrong about guys."

"Yeah, you are." I snicker. "Remember Derek?"

"That doesn't count. He lied about his preferences." She leans into the room and whispers. "Mark my words. That guy is into you."

"No." I shake my head.

"I'll bet you one night alone in the room that he'll be back tomorrow to check on you."

"He won't." Why would he?

"He will."

"Go take your shower," I grumble as I flop back onto my bed. When I remember my beer-soaked clothes, I quickly sit back up and wince at my throbbing ankle. Luckily, my dresser is what's holding up my bed. Reaching down, I pull open the top drawer and grab a sweatshirt, then strip out of my gross tee, the green one that says, "Irish Lass Full of Sass." As soon as that's off, I do my best to get my favorite jeans off as well, but that's not going to happen since they're skinny jeans, and my ankle is too swollen to attempt to get them over that. I decide to get them mostly off, sliding the jeans off my left leg. With one bare leg and the other clad in still-moist jeans, I slip the sweatshirt on and lie back onto the bed. "If I could just get to sleep." I'll wake up and my ankle will be just fine.

3

BECKLYN

"Becklyn?"

I feel my body being jostled a little bit. "No, Mom." She can be so annoying. "Let me sleep."

A deep chuckle causes me to wake a little. "Becklyn." The man's voice is almost a whisper. "Wake up, honey."

"Huh?" I blink a few times and see him standing next to my bed. "Lucky?" Am I dreaming? I've had this dream before. The one where Lucky shows up and climbs into bed with me and does things to me. Lovely, wonderful, nice things....

"I brought some ice. And a wrap for your ankle."

Crap. *That* dream is not *this* dream. This dream is where I made an ass of myself at a party and hurt myself at that same party and the man of my dreams now has to have back surgery because he practically carried me all the way home.

"I don't need back surgery."

Oh. Crap. I said that aloud? What else did I say?

"And you didn't do anything wrong. It was Alex's fault. He fell on top of you."

Now I know I said that entire thing out loud. Deciding to

move on before I recall all the stupid stuff I'd just said, I ask, "Alex?"

"Forward for the basketball team."

"I knew he played basketball." Not really. It was merely an observation that it was possible due the guy's incredible tallness.

"Let me see your ankle." Lucky is already pulling my blanket off me. I don't even consider the fact that all I'm actually wearing is a sweatshirt and undies. Oh, and my jeans, but only on one leg. Which means we're back to the knowledge that all I'm wearing is a top and underwear. When he's got the blanket pulled down past my hips, he stops. "Oh."

Suddenly, I don't care if he sees my thighs. "Here." I throw the blanket the rest of the way off.

"What's with the jeans?" He's staring at my pants.

"Couldn't get them off over the ankle."

Moving back, he turns toward Deena's side of the room. "Can you turn the light on?"

"Sure," she grumbles, adding. "No problem, even though it's freaking late." I hear her footsteps and see the overhead light flick on.

"Jesus," Lucky mutters. "It's huge."

That's what she said.

Don't worry. I'm positive I didn't say *that* out loud.

Pushing up onto my elbows, I look down. "Oh, wow." He's right. It's twice the size it was before.

"No wonder you couldn't get your jeans off." He looks right, then left, then back at me. "Got any scissors?"

"Scissors? What for?"

"To cut off the jeans."

"No." I shake my head. "They're my favorites."

"Becklyn." Lucky's voice suddenly sounds gruff. "We need to get those off."

"Lucky," I whine. "My *favorite* pair. Do you know how long it takes to find the perfect pair of jeans? They're like unicorns."

"I'll get you some new ones."

"You can't just go buy the perfect jeans, Lucky." *Ugh. Guys know nothing.* Those skinny jeans have been a labor of love. They're at just the right spot of not too soft, not too stiff. I've practically babied them to this point. Now, I'll have to start all over with a new pair. "Fine," I agree, because he's right. The ankle of this pair is starting to cut into my skin. "In the top drawer of that desk." I point to the desk closest to me.

Like it's a scene from a horror movie, I watch as Lucky slides the edge of my scissors beneath the hem of my denim. It hurts, but not like the rest of the foot. Squeezing my eyes shut, I hear the sound of the scissors cutting through the fabric. A tearing sound. That's when I open my eyes in time to see the jeans slip down over my swollen ankle.

"There." He tosses the jeans to the floor, reaching over to set the scissors on top of my desk. "Now, let me take a closer look at this ankle." His cool hand slips beneath my foot, the other one underneath my ankle. He lifts gently. "Can you move it?"

I hold my breath and grit my teeth as I first push down, then up. "Good." He smiles at my foot. "It's not broken."

It sure feels broken.

"Here." He places a plastic baggy filled with ice on top of my foot, causing me to shriek.

"A little warning," I squeak. "Geesh."

Lucky chuckles. "After I wrap this up loosely, you can go back to sleep."

"What time is it?"

"One," Deena grouses. "It's tomorrow."

I know why she's saying that. She said he'd "come back tomorrow." Which means she won the bet, which also means I'm going to need to find a place to sleep one night so she can have the room to herself.

"Whatever," I grumble in my defeat.

"Mm-hm."

Ugh. She sounds smug.

"There," Lucky says, patting my knee. "That should help with the swelling." Making eye contact, he gets this stern look on his face. "You need to take it easy tomorrow. Keep ice on it and elevated."

"Yes, Doctor." I giggle.

I suppose it's not that funny. While Lucky isn't a doctor, he is majoring in physical therapy. I don't know exactly what he wants to do after he graduates this May, but whatever it is, it means he won't be here at the U of I anymore. Half of me is scared he's going to move away. Far away. Suddenly, I feel sad. It lasts only a minute, because I'm jolted back to the present when he states, "I'm serious, Becklyn. Stay off the ankle."

"I will."

"I'll be gone all day tomorrow." Deena sighs. "I won't be able to get her the ice she needs."

That's total crap. She'll be here. It's Sunday. That's her day to lie around and watch her reality television shows.

"Oh." Lucky looks down at my foot. "Alright. I'll take care of it."

"No." I shake him off. "Someone on the floor can get me more ice." I place my hand on his. "Seriously, I'll be fine."

"You sure?"

"Positive."

The minute he's out the door, I scowl at Deena. "You're going to give me a little time to heal before you make me sleep outside, right?" I'm not joking. It's a serious question.

"Of course." She rolls her eyes and steps across the room; it falls into darkness as she flips the switch. "And for the record…"

I know what's coming.

"I told you so."

"Uh-huh. It means nothing. He's just being nice because he's my brother's—"

"Why didn't your brother show up?"

"He's mad." I sigh. "When Joe's mad, he stays away."

"You're kidding yourself, Becks. I'm right about this. Wait and see, young grasshopper. Wait and see."

Young grasshopper? WTH?

4

BECKLYN

DEENA WAS WRONG.

I waited. I didn't see a thing. Not Lucky. Not Joe. Nobody. Not for three weeks and counting, because it's been three weeks and two days since my March 17 humiliation. Rest assured, my ankle healed even without the wonderful doctoring of one Lucky Ganetti. It wasn't easy, let me tell you. Take using the bathroom. It was a nightmare hobbling down the long hallway to the one and only bathroom on our floor. Luckily, one of the women who lives on the floor, a volleyball player, loaned me a pair of crutches. Good thing they were adjustable, because that girl is *tall*.

My ankle is better now. Except for a twinge of pain every once in a while, I'm once again a fully functioning college student. It was touch-and-go there for a while. I was this close to renting one of those motorized lark things that you see in the grocery stores, but I decided that'd be bad form. Those scooters are for people who really need them. Besides, I can't afford to rent *anything*.

"I decided I'd like to have the room to myself this weekend."

And here I was thinking Denna forgot about our wager. Guess not. "Saturday, I presume."

Deena giggles like I just said something hilarious. "You *presume*—" She giggles again. "—correctly. There's going to be a rager at the Kappa Kappa Sigma house, and I'm not coming home empty-handed."

What she means is, she's bringing a guy home.

If that's the case, I'll be glad to stay away. No way do I want to be in the same room when she has one of her one-night stands here. Nuh-uh. "Okay." I sigh, wondering where I'm going to go.

"I've got a *genius* idea." She's playing with her ponytail and tapping her foot.

Be afraid. Be very afraid.

Next, she brings her hands up in front of her and taps her fingers together like she's diabolical or something. "You should totally call your brother. You could stay at his place." Winking, she adds, "With you-know-who."

Diabolical. Yes. Genius. No.

"Uh, that's not going to happen." Where would I sleep? There are three bedrooms and three guys. All that remains is his spidery basement and the couch, and I can only imagine what's on that. I shiver, because that thought alone is frightening.

"Just call your bro. He's talking to you again, right?"

I guess she's right. He sent me a text message about a week after the "incident" asking me if I was okay. I responded posthaste that I was, which resulted in his final text. Oh, wait, I guess he sicced my mom on me. He must've called her and told her I was at his party and that I'd gotten myself hurt.

I scoff at the memory. I got *myself* hurt?

I think not.

That's all the fault of that exceptionally tall guy.

Anyhoo, my mom wasn't pleased. But, after I explained that Joe did nothing to help me afterwards and that it was all Lucky, she turned her irritation back onto Joe.

Joe-Schmo: You suck. Mom's pissed at ME now.
See? I know how to play this game.

Me: Sorry.
Me: Not sorry.
Me: You told on me first. Next time keep your trap shut.
Joe-Schmo: You still suck.

After that, no more Joe checking up on me. It's better than nothing, I guess. Deciding to put an end to this conversation, I smile at my roomie. "Don't worry about it, Deena. I'll figure it out." Even if I have to sleep down on the first floor in the lounge, I will.

"Great," she chirps. "I've got my eye on one of the hockey players." She does the diabolical finger thing again. "He's h-a-w-t."

I choose not to go there, because I'm pretty sure she knows how "hot" is actually spelled. "Good for you." I don't really mean that. Well, okay, I want her to be happy. She's a nice person, and we get along really well. It's just, it gets old seeing her get her man All. The. Time. I have no doubt the hockey player in her sights will be in our room on Saturday night. No doubt whatsoever.

"I've gotta go. I'm going to be late for Chem."

"Ugh, Chemistry." She rolls her eyes. "I don't know why you take all those hard classes."

We've been over this several times. I want to be a— Well, I'm not sure what I want to be, but something in the sciences. I don't bother explaining it to her again. Instead, I pick up my book bag and throw it over my shoulder. "See you tonight."

"Sure." She flops back onto her bed. I'm pretty sure she has class too, but I don't bother reminding her. She's an adult. She gets to make her own decisions about her education.

Opening the door, I step out into the hallway and sigh.

"Where the heck will I sleep Saturday?" The entire thing sort of makes me mad. And a little bummed too. But mostly mad. I don't like getting displaced. But a bet is a bet, even though, technically, she was wrong about everything with Lucky. He doesn't "love me." He was just doing the right thing.

"You'll never guess who I ran into today." Deena's smirking. I hate when she does that. She's a social butterfly compared to me —she could've run into anyone, literally. Hell, it could be Liam Hemsworth.

Oh, wow. Can you imagine just bumping into *him*? Talk about an amazing day.

It can't be him, because if she'd met Liam, she would have called me on the spot and had me run to wherever it was so I could meet him too. I mean, that's what friends are for, right?

Okay. Now, I'm getting pissed. If she met Liam Hemsworth and didn't call me…

"Okay, you're doing one of your weird in your head things again."

"Am not." I was.

"Before you think it was someone good, I'll just tell you. It was your brother."

"Joe?"

"Do you have another brother?" I get a dramatic eye roll from her.

"Yes." I do have another brother. His name is Christopher, and he still lives at home, opting out of college so he can pursue his lifelong dream of being a world-renowned bartender.

I'm not kidding. He wants to be a famous mixologist.

When he first told us that, I had to look it up. A mixologist is, well, a fancy bartender.

Her hands are on her hips; she's getting irritated with me. "You know I meant Joe."

"Fine, yes. I know you meant Joe."

"Anyhoo. I told him you were going to be homeless on Saturday, and he said—"

"No." I shake my head. "Why'd you do that?"

Ignoring my question, she keeps right on bulldozing. "And he said you can stay in his room because he's going to be out of town."

"Oh." I have to think about this for a second. Wait. I can stay in Joe's room? I scrunch up my nose, remembering Joe's bedroom back home. It was always dirty and very, very smelly. The guy never changed his sheets, and I highly doubt that's changed. Heck, it's probably worse because he doesn't have my mom breathing down his throat about picking up his crap. Then there are the girls. Nope. Nope. I shake my head. "No way. My brother is gross."

"How bad can it be?" Deena has her hands on her hips, and her face reads: sassy.

"You don't understand. My brother is a disgusting pig. I'll probably get some sort of skin rash from sleeping in his bed." Or an STD, but I'm not going to get into that.

"Clean it up before you sleep there."

I'll have to buy some bleach for sure. And some Brillo pads.

I'd better make a list.

Resigned, I mutter, "Fine."

My response is all Deena needs to do her clapping while she jumps up and down thing.

Do I even need to tell you she was a cheerleader in high school?

"We're all good. Deena's gonna get some and Becklyn won't be sleeping on a strange couch somewhere."

I hate when she talks in third person. It's very unsettling.

5

BECKLYN

It's six o'clock on Saturday night, and I find myself on the front porch of my brother's house. I've knocked twice, but nobody has answered yet. I'd ring the bell, but I know it doesn't work. Raising my hand again, I'm about to knock when a voice startles me. "What're you doing here, Becklyn?"

I turn slowly in search of the owner of the voice.

My favorite voice.

The moment I see him, I feel heat flood my face. It's Lucky, yes. But he's not alone. He's with someone. A girl. Well, a woman. A woman I'd describe as beautiful. Stunning. Nothing like me. "Um..."

The two of them have stopped at the bottom of the front steps. They're both looking up at me. Lucky's eyes pan down to my bag in my right hand and the bucket of cleaning supplies I've got on the ground at my feet. "You gonna clean the place?" Lucky smirks.

"Joe said I could sleep here."

"Excuse me?" It's the woman this time. Her voice is sort of high-pitched. Or maybe it's what she sounds like when she's

29

unhappy. Because if her face is any clue, I'd say she's definitely unhappy

"I— Joe said he was out of town, and because my roommate is entertaining tonight, he said I could sleep here."

The woman looks at Lucky, and back at me. "We thought we had the house to ourselves."

Who is this girl? Woman? We? Ourselves?

Are they a couple?

I didn't know Lucky had a girlfriend.

Deena said he loved me.

I feel heat again, but this time it's behind my eyes. I'm not going to cry over this. I mean, I knew he didn't love me. But still.

"Babe." Lucky looks down at his… whatever she is. "Rain check."

"Lucky?" she whines, and I can't help thinking it's kind of funny. Giggling is out of the question, though, so I hold it in.

At least I try to.

"Who is this"—she glares at me—"big person?"

Big person? I'm sick of people saying stuff like that. I snap, "I'm Joe's sister. Who are *you?*"

She must not like me talking back, because she places her hands on her tiny waist and makes a move to step up onto the porch like she wants to throw down, but Lucky places a palm on her arm. "No."

Ignoring him, she's determined to say, "*I'm* with Lucky."

"Go home, Tiff." Lucky sounds irritated now. I hope it's not directed at me.

"Fine." She spins on her heels. Her four-inch heels. When she gets a few feet away, she turns and glares at me. Looking back at Lucky, she chirps, "Call me."

When our eyes meet, I give Lucky a shrug. "Sorry. I figured Joe would tell you."

"He didn't." Yep. Lucky is absolutely irritated.

"I can go find somewhere else to sleep."

Please say no. Please say no.

"I'm not turning you away, Becklyn."

I pick up my bucket and wait for Lucky to unlock the door. He looks down at my hand. "What's with the cleaning supplies?"

"I'm not sleeping in Joe's room until I clean it." I pretend shiver.

Lucky laughs. It's a nice sound. "Good idea. Joe's a slob."

"I didn't want to catch any communicable diseases."

Another chuckle from Lucky, and I'm beaming with pride. He's doesn't laugh all that often, but when he does, it's notable.

Taking my overnight bag from me, he sets it on top of the dining table. "You eat?"

"No." I brought snacks. They're in my overnight bag, but I'm not about to tell Lucky that.

"I was going to cook…." He flicks his eyes at the door. Which means he was going to cook for Tiff. "Chicken piccata with artichokes."

"Wow, that sounds great." And it does.

"I'll cook while you decontaminate your brother's room."

"Right." Since I've still got the bucket in my hand, I make my way to Joe's room. Sucking in air, I hold my breath and turn the knob. Pushing the door open, I look inside before I take a step. "It's worse than I thought." The smell. Oh, geesh. The smell.

Setting the bucket at my feet, I reach in and pull out the rubber gloves, then snap them into place. Next, I take one of the three rags I brought and a bottle of air freshener. Entering, I begin to spray, moving my arm right, then left, sweeping the entire space.

Standing in a fog of my own making, I hear another chuckle. "At least it smells better already."

"I don't get it." I look around. There are clothes literally everywhere. There's even a shirt hanging from the ceiling fan. "My mom was always on us about keeping our rooms clean." Motioning with the hand that's holding the spray, I keep going. "It's like he's doing the opposite of her teachings."

Lucky chuckles again. "Feel sorry for his wife."

"Huh?" I squeak. "Is he getting married?"

"Uh, no. I mean his future wife."

Glancing at a plate on the floor that looks to have food stuck to it older than me, I wince. "Whoever that poor soul is, she'd better have a strong stomach."

Lucky laughs again. This time a real one. "She'd better."

Bending, I pick up the plate and turn it upside down. The hard clump of what I suspect was pizza at one time, slides off onto the floor and breaks apart like glass. "Petrified."

I hear Lucky slap the doorjamb. "If you want to bring in the dishes as you find them, I'll get them soaking."

"Good plan." I follow him out with the plate and set it on the counter. "Wish me luck." Ha. Luck.

<hr>

"Oh, my god." I'm talking with my mouth full. Sue me. Chewing, swallowing, I look right into Lucky's beautiful eyes. "This is the best food I've ever eaten." No joke.

"Yeah?" he's smiling proudly.

"It is. What are these little green things?" I know they aren't peas because they're sort of tart.

"Capers."

"And artichokes?" I smile as I scoop up more food. "Who knew?" I sure didn't. I don't think I've even eaten an artichoke before. "Good." I take a big bite and chew with a smile. I know, I know. I should be eating with dainty little bites and telling him I'm full after three, but why? Lucky has known me since I was ten. Besides, he likes women like Tiff. And since I'll never be her, I'll just be me.

"I ruined a romantic night with your girlfriend?"

I guess I surprise him with my question. *"Not.* My girlfriend."

"Your date?"

He shrugs. "I guess."

Since I'm not completely clueless, I think what he's saying is Tiff was a hookup. I may as well ask. "Hookup?"

Lucky chokes on his own bite of food. Jumping up, I race to his side of the table and begin patting his back. "You okay?"

Nodding, he waves me off. "I'm good." He laughs. "Jesus, Becklyn. You say the most unpredictable shit."

I'm going to take that as a compliment.

Lucky doesn't address my designation regarding Tiff, so I let it go.

"Where did Joe go this weekend?"

Lucky looks surprised.

"He didn't tell you?"

"No." Why would he? "Deena's the one that arranged all this. She wanted the stupid room to herself so she could…" I clear my throat. "No. He didn't."

Lucky has the look of a man in a quandary. "I'm not sure I should say?"

"Is he in jail or something?" I mean…

"No." He shakes his head. "Job interview."

"Oh?" I guess that makes sense. He's graduating this spring. "Out of town? Chicago?"

"Uh." I've never seen Lucky this conflicted. "San Francisco."

"California?" I squeak. "The West Coast?"

"Yeah."

"Mom's going to shit a brick."

"You need to let him tell her."

"Oh." I raise my hands. "I'm not touching that with a ten-foot pole. That's all on Joe to break the news to Sandy Morrissey." She's literally going to flip. That woman has a thing about family.

She wants us all close. Hell, she'd probably be happy if we all lived with her forever. My dad? Not as much.

"Good plan. Let Joe take the fall."

"No problem." Wow. California. Joe. I suddenly feel sad about it. "I'll miss the disgusting pig."

And I've done it again. I've made Lucky laugh.

Life's good.

Dinner is fun. No. Fun isn't the right word. It's perfect. Lucky has been chatty and pleasant. I think it's the first time since I've known him that we were alone, just the two of us. As soon as we finish eating, Lucky points toward the hall. "Go get done in Joe's room. After I clean up the kitchen, I'm going to head out."

"Oh." I know my face looks like someone just stole all my candy. Someone did. "Where are you going?" I hope it's not to Tiff's house.

"Workout."

"Boxing?"

His back is turned to me as he rinses off our plates. "Yeah."

"Can I come?" Okay. Why did I ask that?

Lucky's head rotates. He's frowning. "*You* want to box?"

Why is that hard to believe? Okay, truth? I just want to watch *him* box, but I guess I could try it. "I'm almost done." I point back to Joe's room. "The sheets are in the dryer. I can't really do a deep clean unless I've got a hazmat suit, and they don't sell those at the CVS. I checked."

I watch his frown turn upside down.

It's beautiful.

His low rumble of a laugh starts up again, and I'm beginning to think it's the best sound in the entire world. Because I know I'm the one that did that. I made Lucky Ganetti laugh.

"You bring something to work out in?"

I look down at my tee and leggings. "Uh." I point to myself. "This outfit is ready for anything."

He chuckles low again as he nods. "Be ready in fifteen minutes."

"Yay!" I do a Deena and clap like a cheerleader. "I'm going to punch some stuff." He laughs again as I run back to Joe's room to find my sneakers.

6

———

BECKLYN

"I'm going to be so good at this," I say as I tap the boxing gloves together in front of me like the professionals. I'm bouncing back and forth from foot to foot like they do there too. "I mean, I'm Irish. And we Irish hold in a lot of anger, which makes us great fighters."

"Is that right?" Lucky chuckles.

"Oh, yeah. Look at all the great Irish boxers…"

Lucky pauses putting his wrap on. He's already got my hands wrapped and a spare set of boxing gloves he had in his locker. They're huge on me, but he said they'd work. When he looks up at me, he arches his brow like he's waiting for me to say something.

"Oh, you want me to name one?" I give him my best smile. "There's the greatest pugilist ever from back in the eighteenth century… Shaun O'Shaughnessy."

His smile is instantaneous. It's big, and he's even showing teeth.

Win.

"Shaun O'Shaughnessy?" Lucky's full on laughing now.

"And let's not forget about Donal McDougall."

"Jesus." Lucky shakes his head, still laughing. "You're crazy, Becklyn."

"Crazy like a *fox*." I punch my hands together again and bounce from foot to foot. Gah! I can't wait to hit something. "Ooh," I say with a gleam. "That could be my boxing name. The Irish Fox."

Tapping the top of my head with his boxing glove, he says, "Alright, Foxy. Show me what you've got."

Lucky takes me to the back of the large, open gym space to a boxing bag that's suspended from the ceiling. He demonstrates how to stand, with my feet apart, one of them back a little bit to give me support. I do as he instructs. "Like this?"

"Yeah, but…" He leans down and taps my right knee with his glove. "Move this one back a little." Once I'm set up, he shows me how to jab. He starts off slow but speeds up until his fists move so fast you hardly see his movements. "Now you."

"Okay." I sigh. Stepping closer to the bag, I check my feet again, hold the gloves up in front of my face like he did, and I punch the bag. Hard.

"Good job," Lucky says with a smile. "Now, do it again three times in a row, like this." Bam-bam-bam. I hear his glove make contact with the bag in rapid succession.

Getting back into position, I do it. I hit the bag three times as fast as I can.

"Slow down. Form is more important than speed. You don't want to hit the bag the wrong way; you could hurt yourself." He nods at the bag. "Try it again."

I do as he says, I punch the bag. Once he's satisfied with my form, he moves over to his own bag, while I hit mine about a million times with my right hand—after which he tells me to do the same with my left.

By the time I'm done, I'm sweaty and certain I'm going to be sore tomorrow, but it was fun. Actually, it was the most fun I've ever had working out. Pulling off the gloves, I take a seat on a bench not far from where Lucky is working out. He's punching his own bag, but his workout is nothing like mine, because he's punching and moving around the bag like he's dancing with the thing. It's incredible.

When he sees me, he stops suddenly and smiles. At me. A big smile like the one earlier. I take a moment to stare at his teeth. I've always thought he had the best smile. It's not perfect, mind you. He's got one tooth on the top that's a little crooked, which only makes his smile more endearing.

"You done?"

I'm jerked from my thoughts at his question. Shrugging, I say, "I guess."

His expression changes to something expectant. "You like it?"

"I did. I really liked it." Standing up, I move closer to his bag. "It's the most fun I've ever had working up a sweat."

Lucky's face suddenly morphs. His eyes get round, and I swear he's blushing.

What?

What'd I say?

"Maybe I can come again?"

Lucky suddenly turns and walks over to his gym bag.

What?

What'd I say?

"Lucky?"

"Yeah?" he's bent over, reaching for his water bottle.

What was I going to say? *Think of something, Becklyn.* "Are you finished?"

He chokes on the water, and I cannot for the life of me figure out what his deal is.

Nodding, he says to the ceiling like he can't look at me—God, am I hideous? I bet I am. I tend to sweat a lot—"My workout is complete, yes."

What a weird thing to say. "Can I come again?" Maybe I shouldn't be asking. Is it rude?

"Sure." Lucky looks back at me. "Sure."

"Good." I smile as I hand him back his gloves.

"Keep 'em." He nods down at my hands. "Keep the wrap too. If you want to work out again, you might as well hang on to them."

"Thanks, Lucky."

BACK AT THE HOUSE, LUCKY JUMPS IN THE SHOWER FIRST. WHILE he does that, I definitely don't spend several minutes imagining what he looks like all wet and soapy. And naked. No sirree. I don't think about it at all. Instead, I grab Joe's sheets from the dryer. When I lay the fitted sheet out on his bed, I grimace, because I can't believe Joe would sleep on them the way they were. Case in point, when I put them in the washer, the sheets were brownish tan. Now, they're gray. I suspect they were white when they started out. Mom would've had a fit if she'd seen his room.

"Damn."

"What's wrong?" Still holding onto the sheet, I whip around to see Lucky wearing only a towel. Water droplets are clinging to his chest for dear life.

Lucky droplets...

I know if I were one of those water drops, I'd do whatever I could to stay right there. Well, maybe I'd slide on down....

"Oh." I clear my throat, because it's suddenly as dry as the Sahara Desert. My face is hot too, which means I've got to be as pink as a flamingo. And not in a good way. "Uh..." *Spit it out, Becklyn.* "I was thinking I should've taken some blackmail pics of his room."

"Blackmail?" he smiles. "Your mom?"

"Yep." Turning away from the hottest man on earth, I start to make the bed. "She'd let him have it."

"Mrs. M is one tough cookie."

"You know," I turn back to him, "you can call her Sandy." Actually, she used to ask him to call her Mom, since he didn't have one. His dad, John, grew up in our hometown and knew my dad when he was young. Lucky's grandparents still live there, or they did. His grandma passed away a few years ago, and his grandpa is in a home now. They were nice people. As for John Ganetti, well, he's an acquired taste, I guess you could say. Growing up, I couldn't help but be a little scared of him. He was always angry. At least that's the way he seemed to me. It's probably why Lucky spent so much time at our house. Why wouldn't he? My mom is nice, and my dad is hilarious.

"I know." Lucky shrugs. "Just used to calling her Mrs. M."

"You call my dad Billy."

Lucky smirks. "Everyone calls him Billy."

He's right. Dad insists on it. I asked him about it once, and he says it makes him feel young. He hates to be called Mr. Morrissey, and he's a dang high school teacher. It's usually frowned upon to call a teacher by his first name, but he's been at it a long time; nobody at school cares if the students call him Billy.

"True."

There's a moment of silence between us. Lucky's standing in the doorway in his towel, I'm clutching Joe's sheet, and we're just looking at each other. I'm not sure who breaks the silence first.

Me.

It was me.

"Wanna watch something?"

I mean, it's Saturday night, and it's not even ten yet.

"Sure." He looks down at himself. "You gonna take a shower, Foxy? You really worked up a sweat."

I'd already forgotten my boxing moniker. It makes me laugh. "Yep."

"I'll get dressed and meet you in the living room in fifteen."

"Great."

I'm in and out of the shower in minutes. And it's not because

I'm excited to watch TV with Lucky. Well, part of it is. The other part? Their bathroom is disgusting. I had to grab one of the cleaners I brought to scrub out the shower floor before I stepped inside. I'm amazed none of these guys has a foot fungus.

It gives me pause. *Maybe they do.*

I quickly dress and make a plan to clean the entire bathroom in the morning. It's the least I can do. For their health.

In the living room, I smile at the sight before me. Lucky on the couch, his feet propped up on the coffee table, and a big bowl of popcorn in his lap. "Ooh, popcorn." I rub my hands together.

"No butter." He winks. "Just like you like it."

I flush at his words. The fact that he remembered that I hate butter on my popcorn makes me feel… funny. Happy, though. Shaking it off, I move to the couch and sit next to him. I reach into the bowl and grab a handful.

"Shower good?"

I stop with my hand about an inch from my face. Giving him my best stink eye, I say, "After I scrubbed the shower floor."

"You cleaned the shower?"

Leaning forward, I look at Lucky's feet. He's not wearing socks. Weird. Who knew feet could be sexy? I mean, I feel tingles just from the sight of them. They're big, like the rest of him, but well groomed. Clipped toenails, and no hair on his toes like both my brothers' feet. Theirs look like Chewbacca feet. Not Lucky's, though.

"What're you looking at?" He's leaning forward now, looking at his feet too.

"Just wondering if you have any fungus."

"Huh?" He sounds startled.

"That shower?" I shake my head. "Disgusting. I'm shocked you don't have green feet."

Once again, I hear him laugh. Sitting up straight, I look over at him. He's really laughing this time. His head is back, and I watch his Adam's apple move up and down. Sexy. Very sexy. "Jesus, Foxy…"

And that's when I smile, because not only have I made him laugh a bunch today, I've now got a nickname—one just between Lucky and me, and there's nothing, and I mean nothing, better than that.

7

BECKLYN

WHEN I WAKE THE NEXT MORNING, HE'S GONE. TO SAY I'M disappointed, well, that's an understatement. I mean, we had such a good time last night. He chose the movie—a war movie, which was such a guy thing to pick. Not only that, it was boring as heck, but it didn't matter because I was watching it with *him*. Rest assured, I know all there is to know about the first world war now. Not true but it feels that way.

Anyway, when I get up, I tiptoe to the bathroom to check myself in the mirror. I don't want him to see me like—well—like me in the morning, which is quite scary. I peek in the living room first. He isn't there. Next, the kitchen. Not there either. What I do find is a note.

Becklyn,
> *Had stuff to do. See you around.*
> *-L*

And that's it. Not gonna lie, I'm disappointed he didn't address me as Foxy. Maybe that was just a thing from last night.

Why am I bummed out? What did I expect? He's busy. He's a

senior here at U of I. He's a physical therapy major, and that takes lots of time, because in addition to classes, he does stuff at a clinic here in town as part of his degree. That's what Joe told me once, anyway. It makes sense.

Yeah, he's busy. Too busy to hang with me all weekend.

Besides. I'm busy too. My paper for Comp 106 isn't going to write itself.

———

I'VE BARELY GOT MY FOOT IN THE DOOR WHEN DEENA ASKS, "HOW was it?"

"Fine." I arch my brow. "How 'bout you? Did you get the guy?"

"Yeah?" she shrugs. "Nothing to phone home about."

She's talking about the sex.

"Sorry." I'm not sure Deena is ever happy with the sex afterwards. Maybe if she did the sex with someone she actually cared about…. That's none of my business, though. And since I've never had *the sex*, I'm probably not the right person to speculate about the reasons she's never satisfied with her partners.

Wow, that was a lot. What I just said there.

It was a confession, of sorts. Not that you're surprised, right? I mean, I mentioned earlier that I've never had a boyfriend.

And believe me, I'm one of those people who wants to do *it*. I just prefer the first time to be with someone I love. Sue me.

"Well, I've got a ton of homework. Gonna head to the library."

"Booooooring."

I roll my eyes, but she can't see. "I know. School is such a drag."

"Right?"

I giggle, because the girl makes me laugh. "You could come with me?" I'm sure she's got homework.

She crinkles up her nose, and it's adorable. How does she do that? Look adorable with a scrunched-up face? "I'd rather go to the mall, but thanks."

Me too. But no money and no time means no mall.

"Want to go down to dinner together later?"

"Sure." She gives me her brightest smile. "Six?"

"Perfect." At my desk, I gather up my laptop and books and stuff them into my bookbag. After that, I'm out the door.

8

BECKLYN

"Hey, Foxy."

That voice… he used my nickname.

I look up and blink at the sight of him all gorgeous in a hoody and jeans. Seriously. The man can make an ancient hoody look amazing.

I sigh because… *God, he's beautiful.*

"Whatcha doin'?" He nods at my laptop.

"Writing a riveting paper comparing and contrasting the benefits of electric cars versus the internal combustion engine."

"Really?" He looks surprised.

"Really."

"And?" He slides into the seat across from me. "What's your conclusion?"

"Obviously, the electric car." I'm taking a class in Environmental Science thinking this might be a good major for me. We'll see. So far, I'm not sure it's my thing.

"Obviously. But why? I've heard some negative things about the batteries used in electric cars."

He's right. Lucky and I spend a good twenty minutes talking

about renewable energy. Honestly, I'm surprised how much he knows about it.

I take that back. I'm *not* surprised. Lucky is uber smart. No doubt he could kick some ass in a trivia contest, because he reads a ton and soaks up lots of interesting facts about everything. Plus, he watches old war movies for fun. That should tell you all you need to know.

"You wanna get a bite to eat?"

I'm not sure I'm hearing him right. "Eat?"

"Yeah, you know. Dinner? We could go to the Student Center."

As if on cue, my stomach growls. All I've eaten today are some oldish cheese crackers that were in the front pocket of my backpack. "Oh, sure." I smile. "Great." The two of us stare at each other for a second. "Oh. Now?"

"Now is good, Foxy. It's dinnertime."

"Right." I save my document, shut my laptop, and slide everything back into my bookbag. Standing, I heave it over my shoulder and grunt.

"Here." He takes my bag from me and slides it over his shoulder. "Damn. No wonder you were wincing. This thing weighs a ton."

"I'm used to *that*." I point to my bag. "I'm a little sore from boxing."

"You okay?" He looks concerned, and it's sweet as heck.

"Sure." I smile. "I just worked some muscles that haven't seen the light of day in a while."

Lucky nods as we start the trek to the student center. Several people wave at Lucky. A couple of girls actually touch him as they stroll by, and for some reason, that really bugs me. "Do people just come up and run their hands on you like that?"

"People?"

"You know I mean girls." Cue eyeroll.

"Some of them do."

"Doesn't it bug you?"

He shrugs. "Nah." He looks down at me. "Does it bug *you*?"

"You mean when I see girls touching you?" Should I answer that?

"No. When guys do that to you?"

I snicker at his ridiculous question. "You mean when *all* the guys walk by and grope me?" Sarcasm. Priceless.

Stopping in his tracks, Lucky turns. "Guys have been groping you?" He looks around central campus like he's looking for a killer. "Who the fuck has been groping you?"

Reaching out, I touch his forearm. God, even that is made of rippling muscles. "Nobody, Lucky." I release a nervous laugh. "Nobody is groping me. I was just kidding."

With a look that tells me he's not sure he believes me. I roll my eyes. "Who's gonna grope *me*, Lucky?" Seriously. *Who?*

"Knock it off, Becklyn. You're gorgeous, and you know it." Lucky turns back in the direction of the student center and starts walking again.

He thinks I'm gorgeous?

The Student Center is that building on campus with lots of little businesses inside. Like a copy center where you can make copies (obviously), but also bind books (I'm not really sure when I'd ever need to bind a book but I know where to go if I do.), and make posters. The university bookstore is also housed in the Student Center, along with a food court kind of place with a bunch of different food stations with everything from pasta to sushi. The minute we walk in, Lucky picks up two trays and hands me one. "I'm fucking starving. Meet you at the register?" He looks back at me expectantly.

"Sure." *Phew.* Thank goodness. I'm not sure why the idea of Lucky walking around this place with me makes me nervous. It's not like he hasn't seen me eat. Nonetheless, I decide to make good food choices, and not because Lucky's with me. Because after boxing with him yesterday, I feel better, physically. Sore, for sure, but better. At the salad bar, I make myself a small side salad with lots of veggies. At the grill station, I order up a grilled chicken sandwich. I'm very tempted to get fries but I decide on fresh fruit instead. Looking down at my tray, I smile with pride. My dinner looks both nutritious and delicious. Stopping at the condiment station, I load up on dill pickles and add a little barbecue sauce to my chicken sandwich but skip the mayo.

"That looks good." Lucky eyes my tray when steps up next to me in the checkout line. "I should have gotten the grilled chicken." He stares down at his tray. It's heaping with what looks to be fried rice and vegetables. On the side he's got a cup of soup and a salad.

"I'll share."

Looking at the food stations, he looks back at me. "Nah. If I'm still hungry, I'll come back for seconds."

I guess I can't argue with that logic.

After we pay for our food using our U-cards (those are like debit cards but for school purchases), I follow him to a booth near the back wall. We sit opposite one another, and I smile to myself, thinking how perfect this is. Lucky and me having dinner together. Twice in one week. I'm about to ask him about his day when two women approach our table. There's a tall brunette and a blonde I recognize. Tiff.

Tiff slides into the booth on Lucky's side. She's so close, I'm surprised there's enough room for air to pass between them. "Hey, Lucky," she says in a syrupy sweet voice. "Long time, no see."

She saw him yesterday.

hard eye roll

Granted, it wasn't for very long, but that's not my fault.

Yes, it is.

"Uh-huh." He's got his fork in his hand poised to dig into his rice. I know he's hungry. He said so.

"I'm sad we didn't get to have our evening together." She sticks out her bottom lip in a pout, all while she glares at me.

He's staring down at his plate. I'd bet you a hundred bucks he's not really listening to her. He's only thinking of the food in front of him. I want to laugh, but that'd be wrong. Right? Instead, I take my chicken sandwich in hand, lean down, and take a big bite. Chewing, I make a yummy sound. That's when Lucky's eyes find mine. I smirk as I chew because the look on his face is priceless. Nodding, I smile. "Good sandwich."

"Do you have to be that noisy when you eat?" Tiff snaps. "You sound disgusting."

I set my food down and give her a glare of my own. Just as I say, "Excuse me?" Lucky says, "Thanks for stopping by, Tiffany. I'll see you around."

"B-but," she sputters, "what about...?"

"I said I'll see you around." Lucky isn't having any of it. And I love it.

"Fine." She slides back out of the booth. Standing near the table, she gives me a look that could kill. With a fake-as-heck smile, she lifts her hand and waves with just her fingers. "Byeee."

"Later," Lucky grumbles.

When the two women are gone, he looks at me. "Sorry about her."

I shrug. "Haters gonna hate."

Lucky laughs. It's a sound I could really get used to.

9

BECKLYN

Using my key, I unlock my dorm room door. Pushing it open, I notice it's dark inside.

Weird.

Stepping inside, I reach for the light and flip the switch. When I turn, I jump because Deena's on her bed, back against the wall, arms crossed. The sight startles the bejeezus out of me, but it's the look on her face that really gives me shivers.

She's pissed.

I learned early on that when she's angry, it's best just to get to the bottom of it. "What's wrong?" I ask, because it's hard to tell with her. She gets angry a lot. It could be anything from me forgetting to unplug my flat iron to drinking the last diet soda. Soda that *I* purchased, by the way.

"What's wrong?" she asks, the anger evident in her voice. "I've been sitting here since six o'clock waiting for you."

Six o'clock?

"We were supposed to meet and go to dinner together. Remember?"

No. Oh, crap. Yes. "I'm sorry." I really am. "I forgot."

"Obviously." She slides off her bed and walks past me bumping my shoulder as she goes. "I can't believe you forgot."

"I'm sorry. You should've gone without me."

"You know I hate that place. Every clique in the world hangs out in the dining hall."

It's true. But that hasn't stopped her before. "You could've sent me a text?" Weak response, I know. I can't believe I forgot, honestly. Oh, wait, yes I can. "Lucky—"

She whips around suddenly. "What about Lucky?"

"He asked me to eat with him at the Student Center."

"He did?" Her voice is no longer angry. "And you went?"

"Well." *Duh.* "Yeah."

Moving back to her bed, she sits on the edge and leans forward. I'm sensing some of her anger is gone. "Start at the beginning. Tell me everything."

I smile because I'm relieved this particular round of angry Deena has been short-lived. She's been known to stay mad for several days. I hate that. "I was at the library."

She uses her hand to urge me to move faster.

"He stopped by my table and asked me if I was hungry." Or something like that.

"Did you walk together, or did he meet you there?"

"We walked together."

"And what did you eat? Please don't tell me you chose something like spaghetti."

"What's wrong with spaghetti?"

"Messy and slurpy-sounding." She nods encouraging. "Go on."

Deena thinks of things I never would. *Slurpy?* "Grilled chicken sandwich and salad."

Her hands move to her face suddenly. "Oh, grasshopper…"

I still don't know what "grasshopper" means, but I'm hoping she's not about to chastise me.

"I'm damn proud." She's smiling from ear to ear. "I've taught you well. You chose the perfect things. You didn't eat the bun, though, right?"

"Uh, right." Hell yes, I ate the bun.

"Okay. Sorry." She places her hands on her lap. "Keep going."

I do. I tell her about Tiff and eating and well, that's about it. "After we ate, we walked out of the Student Center. He turned right, and I went left."

"Did he try to hold your hand or anything?"

"No. Why would he do that?"

Deena's head flops back as she releases an exasperated breath. Looking back at me, she says, "Because he loves you, silly."

"He doesn't." He likes me. I guess. As a friend. "We're just friends."

"For now." That's when I hear her stomach growl.

"You didn't eat?" I look at the clock. It's just after eight. "You still have time." The cafeteria for our dorm doesn't close until nine.

"Oh, I'll just eat something here."

All we have are old granola bars and some saltines.

"I'll go down with you."

She shakes her head. "Everything will be picked over."

"There will be *ice cream*." I sing "ice cream." Half the time, that's what Deena gets for her entree anyway.

"True." She gives me a devious little smile.

"Come on."

* * *

"You know what you should totally do now?"

"What?" This ought to be good. Deena's always got new ways to make me do stupid stuff.

"You should stop over at your brother's place and ask him about his job interview."

There's no need for that. He already sent me a text thanking me for cleaning his room. In my response to him, I told him he'd better spill the beans to Mom about his interview or I was going to use it against him. His response? "LOL"

I guess he doesn't fear Mom like I do.

He should.

"I don't need to do that."

"Need?" she scoffs. "This isn't about *need*, silly Becklyn. This is about creating opportunities to see *that man*. That hot, hot man."

She's right about one thing. I would like to see him again. "I'd like to start boxing."

"Like punching stuff?" Even her frown is pretty.

"Yes. It was fun." And a good workout. "And Lucky boxes."

"Oh." She smiles slyly. "I get it."

She doesn't. Not really.

"Where does he work out?"

"Smith's Gym."

"I've heard of that place. I think they have fitness classes there too." She taps her chin. "Hang on." She reaches into her purse for her phone. I watch as she taps away. "Ooh, they have a student special."

I probably can't afford it no matter how special the special is.

"Buy one membership, get one free."

"Wow." That's a good special.

"I'll join, and you can go for free."

Deena can definitely afford to join. Her allowance from her parents is ridiculous. Still. "No." I shake my head. "That's not—"

She holds up her hand to stop me. "Just make sure I'm your maid of honor when you marry Lucky Ganetti."

"Sure." This time, I let her see my eye roll. She's insane. Well, okay. Yes, I've fantasized about marrying Lucky, but that's all it is. A fantasy.

"We'll go first thing in the morning." Deena's already planning. Only one problem.

"I've got class."

Slapping the table lightly, she snaps, "You always have class. God. That gets so tiresome."

I want to laugh, but I'd better not. "I'm done at noon. Can we go after that?"

"I guess." She sounds put off, but that turns into a bright smile and there's now a chirp to her voice. Clapping like she just got a new puppy, she adds, "This is *exciting*. Ooh." She stops clapping. "I'll go buy myself something cute to wear while you're at class."

"Good idea." Trust me. Deena has plenty of cute workout clothes. But one more outfit won't hurt, I guess.

1 0

BECKLYN

"WHAT ARE YOU DOING HERE, BECKLYN?"

I look up from my spot on the floor. The kickboxing instructor told us to lie on our backs and do something called crunches.

I already hate crunches.

I blink up at Lucky and can't help noticing, well, everything. His stance. It's one I've seen many times. Arms crossed. And is he tapping his foot at me? I can't worry about that; instead I take notice of his clothes. Baggy athletic shorts and a tight black T-shirt with the sleeves cut off revealing his unbelievable arms and those shoulders. Gah. He's got big, round shoulders that flex with muscles when he moves. His whole look is good on him, because even though the shorts are baggy, they still hang just right.

"Becklyn," he repeats, sounding peeved. "I asked you a question."

It's an odd question, really. Can't he see I'm working out? I mean, he must've seen me through the window. The one that looks out onto the main floor of the huge gym. Then, he came inside where the Introduction to Kickboxing class is currently taking place.

61

Quickly, I glance up to the front at our instructor. I learned pretty quickly that the woman running the class wants our full attention. If she doesn't have it, she yells.

Whispering, I say, "I'm in class." Pointing up to our angry little leader, I add, "Don't get me into trouble with Stalin up there."

"Foxy." Lucky sounds amused but also serious. "Answer my question."

"She's working out," Deena pipes up from somewhere behind me. "Duh."

Pointing at the door, he says, "When you're done, I want to talk to you."

"Sure." My turn to point at the door. "Now go before you seriously get me into trouble."

"You," the instructor shouts as she points right at me. "Why aren't you doing crunches?"

"See?" My turn to get snippy with him. "Go." I point toward the door again.

He glares at me, but he goes.

***

"That was intense," Deena says as soon as we're out of the room.

Of course, she still looks perfect in her entirely pink outfit. Heck, even her new tennis shoes are pink. I look down at myself and frown. I'm wearing black workout leggings and a huge gray T-shirt with the words "I'm Not For Everyone" on the front. I splurged on it when I saw it because it made me laugh. Plus, it came in a 3X, which means it's nice and baggy, hanging long, practically down to my knees. In other words, it's perfect. I'm also dripping with sweat. I glance at Deena again and wonder if she actually exercised. Her hair is still perfect. Mine is soggy and hanging down into my face. The back of my neck is wet with sweat, and I feel it still running down my back. It's gross. But do you know what? I feel really good. I know I look like crapola, but I don't care.

"How was it?" Lucky says from right behind me. He's close; he can probably smell me.

Ick. *Now*, I care. I slowly turn to face him.

Bad idea.

My front looks way worse than my back.

"Wow." He smirks. "You really got a workout, huh?"

Kill me now.

"It was super-duper intense." Deena says sidling up next to me. She's dabbing her cheeks gently with her little pink towel.

Lucky pretty much ignores her and looks back at me. "You should've told me you wanted to join. I could've gotten you a discount. I know the owner."

"Oh," Deena giggles. "They had a special."

I point my thumb at her. "Buy one, get a free membership. She bought one, I got a free one."

Lucky frowns for a second. "Wow. That's, uh, a good deal."

"It is." I nod. "Yeah, anyway, I loved punching stuff..." I shrug. "I figured—why not?"

"You still should've told me."

"Why?" I'm not intentionally being obtuse. I really want to know.

"It's a free country, Lucky. Why? Did she need to ask your permission to join?" Deena's catching the same vibe from him that I am. It's weird.

He glances at Deena, then back at me. "All I meant was, if you'd told me, *I* could have shown you how to do some of those kickboxing moves."

Deena makes an exasperated sound. "It's kicking and punching. What's hard about that?"

Lucky's voice changes. He sounds downright pissed as he directs his next words at her. "If you don't have your feet planted right, you could strain your back. If you don't use proper form when you hit, you can pull muscles." He's glaring at Deena. When I glance at her, all she's doing is smirking.

She throws her arm over my shoulders. I should warn her that she's going to get my sweat on her, but she doesn't flinch. With a shrug, she says, "I guess you're right. We can't have our sweet little Becklyn getting hurt."

I half expect Lucky to correct her, but he doesn't. Instead, he merely nods. Looking back at me, he doesn't sound mad anymore. "You can come with me later this week. I'll help you out."

That's not necessary. But I'm not about to tell him that. "Oh. Okay."

Deena is cracking me up now, because she says, "That's very kind of you, but I won't be able to make it this week. It'll have to be just the two of you."

Lucky arches one brow at her. "Right." At me, he adds, "How 'bout Friday night, Foxy?"

"Friday?" I have to think what I've got going on, but it's hard when he's so near. Why does he have to smell that good? "I—"

"Of course. Friday will be perfect," Deena answers for me.

"Yeah." I nod. "Okay."

"Pick you up at five." He starts to turn. "We can get some dinner afterwards."

"Sure." I nod again like an idiot. "Okay."

The second he's out of sight, Deena starts to cackle. "Oh. My. God. He's *so* in love with you."

"He's not." *Is he?*

Grabbing my arm, she starts to pull me toward the front door. "We're going to get you a new workout outfit. You can't go on your date looking like a bog monster."

What the heck is a bog monster? "It's not a date."

She halts suddenly. "He's picking you up. On a Friday. You're doing something. After which, you're going to dinner. That, my sweet, naïve friend, is a date."

"It's not." I mean it. It's not a date. "He thinks he's my brother."

"Bullshit," she spits, pulling me along again. "Your brother could care less if you 'strained something' kicking a stupid bag."

She's right about that.

"Mark my words, grasshopper. That man back there…" She uses her thumb to point back to the building. "…loves you."

If only that were true.

11

BECKLYN

Ever since Deena told me this was a date, I've been a nervous wreck. I can barely concentrate on my schoolwork, and I've hardly eaten. I've tried, but every time I'm about to put something in my mouth, I get a little queasy.

Now that it's Friday and this thing is about to happen, I'm *really* queasy.

"Come on. Let me fix your hair." Deena has gone above and beyond to get me ready for this thing. We went to a discount store to find me something to wear. Luckily, the place had some decent-looking things for cheap. I'm wearing black, because it's the most slimming. I've got on workout leggings, a long black V-neck tee with long sleeves, and a matching fitted zip-up jacket. I look put together while still feeling like I'm covered.

I move over to her side of the room, where she's standing holding a hairbrush and a scrunchie. "A high ponytail would look adorable."

I remain silent as she does her work. She even talked me into wearing a little makeup, even after I told her it was just going to run down my face thanks to the sweat. Her response? "Well, don't sweat."

She makes it sound so simple.

"Here." She hands me her black metal water bottle. "Drink lots of water."

As soon as she's got my hair done, there's a knock on the door. Deena gasps with excitement. "This is it. Your first date with Lucky Ganetti."

Wow. Maybe she's right. It certainly feels like a date.

"Remember." She sounds serious. "Be yourself."

"Okay." I nod like I know what the heck she means. How could I be anyone else?

"Try to touch his arm every once in a while."

I nod again.

"And giggle a lot."

Wait. I thought she told me to be myself?

When the knock on the door becomes more insistent, she breaks away from me. Reaching for the door, she turns to me and says, "Ready?"

No, but I nod anyway. I force a smile onto my face even though I want to puke. I watch her turn the knob and pull the door open while stepping away. The minute I see the man standing in my doorway, my face falls.

Like a ton of bricks.

"You ready, dipshit?"

Joe.

"Where's Lucky?" Deena is the one to ask, thank goodness.

Joe glances at Deena and back at me. "In the car. Let's go. I'm fucking starving, and we've got to do some shit at the gym before I can eat."

I feel a burning sensation behind my eyes and in my nose. I know what it means. It means tears are imminent.

Deena steps up to me. With an expression that screams pity, she pats my arm. "Go on." She nods to the door. "Go have fun."

"Right." I give her my fakest smile. "Fun."

As I step toward the door, my brother asks, "Why the hell are you all dolled up? You're going to get all sweaty." He chuckles. "You sweat like a damn pig when you exert yourself even the slightest."

Leave it to my brother to say the absolutely wrong thing. Because the first tear falls before I can stop it.

"What the hell's wrong with you?" Joe is such a stupid jerk. "Why are you crying?"

I say the first thing that comes out of my mouth. "Cramps." I know it's the exact right thing to say, because my brother hates when my mom and I mention anything about our periods.

"No." He shakes his head. "You know there's no talking about your girl problems." He's glaring at me now. "You're gonna bitch and moan about that shit all night, aren't you?"

In the past, I've only done that to Joe for a laugh. It's fun to make him uncomfortable. "You're right. I'd better just stay home."

"Agreed." He nods and turns on his heel and heads out of my room, adding, "See ya" as he goes.

Wiping away a couple more tears, I look at my friend and roommate. "I couldn't."

"I don't blame you, hon." She wraps her arms around me. "I'm sorry I got you excited about a date."

"No. I knew it wasn't." I did. I really did. I just chose to believe her.

"Why is your brother such an asshole?"

I shrug, still wrapped up in her hug. "He's always been a jerk."

"He's next-level jerk."

"He really is."

12

———————

BECKLYN

I haven't felt like doing much lately. Even going to class has been a challenge. I've gone but I haven't been engaged. Not really.

Strange how depression can just come up on you like that. One minute you're excited about life and the possibilities it holds. The next, all you want to do is sleep.

And eat.

"Oh. My. *Gahhhd.*"

Here we go. Deena.

"What?" I know what, but I might as well let her vent.

"I'm sick of this."

"Sick of what?"

"Of you." She points to me. "All this moping. I'm over it. Get your ass up. We're going to the gym."

"Uh. No. I'm not going to the gym." No way. I'm not stepping foot into that place ever again.

"Yes." She places her hands on her stupidly tiny hips. "We are."

"No. I'm not." I nod at the door. "You go." Geesh. She's getting on my last nerve. Everybody knows someone with a broken heart

71

just wants to be left alone, but not Deena. No. Deena keeps hovering. Pestering.

"Get. Up." She's sounding sort of snippy now.

I guess repeating myself is what I'm doing today. "I'm not going. You go. Leave me in peace."

Deena turns like she's going to the door, but that's not what she does. I watch her arms go up and her hands cover her face. I can see her shoulders slumping at first; they're shaking. Is she laughing at me? When she suddenly turns to face me, she lowers her hands, and that's when I see she's definitely not laughing. She's crying.

"Deena? What's wrong?" This woman never cries.

"I'm scared."

"Scared? About what?"

"You."

"Me?"

"Yes. *You.* I've never seen you like this. So down. I can't take it. I've tried to think of ways to make you feel better."

And she has tried. She's offered to stay home from a night out after I refused to go, to watch movies with me, she's said the word "makeover" about twenty times this week, and now she thinks going to the place where *he* goes is going to make me feel better.

It's not.

"That's when I finally realized what you need."

"Which is?"

"Punching something. Hard."

Don't forget kicking something. Like Lucky's face. And my brother's, for that matter.

Maybe she's right. Maybe what I need to do is get out of bed. Put on some clean clothes. I stare at Deena for a minute or two. "I'll go—"

"Yay." She claps and bounces up and down.

"If." I hold up my finger. "We drive past Lucky's house like ninjas to see if he's home. If he's home…" I'll know he's not at Smith's Gym. "I'll go to the gym."

"Deal." She turns to my dresser, opens up the second drawer, and pulls out a tee. "Put this on. That one"—she points at me—"is disgusting."

It is. It really is, because I have been changing back into the same clothes as soon as I walk in the door from class for several days. It can't be helped.

Reluctantly, I throw back my comforter and slide out of bed. Weird. I'm sore. Even more slowly, I take the shirt from Deena and search for my sports bra.

Behind me, she claps three times. "Chop, chop. Class is in twenty minutes. If you want to drive by your brother's place, you'll need to get the lead out."

"I'm hurrying."

<hr>

"The coast is clear," Deena whispers to me from up ahead.

We drove by my brother's place, and Lucky's car was parked on the street. Without even discussing it, Deena drove us straight to the gym. I let her walk in first. I don't know why I'm still tentative.

Once we find a spot in the back of class that lets us see what the instructor is doing and sort of hides us from her wrath, I feel myself relax a little bit.

He's not here.

Which is essential, because I'm not ready to face him.

I shouldn't be angry with him. He did nothing wrong, really. I'm just embarrassed. I got myself all excited that Lucky Ganetti actually liked me. It's not Deena's fault, either. Sure, she encouraged it, but it's all on me for believing something so far-fetched. I scoff to myself. Because people like beautiful Lucky Ganetti don't go for people like me, plain, boring Becklyn Morrissey. Instead, they go for the Tiffs of the world.

"Let's get started," the instructor shouts from the front. And for the first time in a week, I feel something other than sad. Because I'm about to kick the crap out of this bag. That thought alone makes me happy.

As soon as the hour-long class is over, I'm bent at the waist, panting. Sweat is dripping off me like I'm made of water. "Wow," I say between gasps. "That was something."

"Feel better?"

"I do." No lie. I feel much better.

She reaches out to pat my shoulder but must think twice about touching my sweaty self, because she winces and pulls back. I get an encouraging smile instead. "You did great."

"Thanks."

As we head out of the room, I'm wiping off my face when a male voice says, "What're you doing here, squirt?"

I'd recognize Joe's voice anywhere, because the guy only has one volume. Loud.

"What's it look like?" I sneer at him because I'm still mad. I know. I know. It's not his fault, probably.

"It looks like you look like shit." He snickers. "You're sweating like a damn pig." God. I want to punch his smug face. Thanks to my class, I know how to do it now too. Curling up my fist at my side, I'm tempted to do a jab-cross on his stupid butt when there's another voice.

"Hey, Becklyn."

Glancing to my left, my eyes meet Lucky's. "Oh." I smile at him but it's a painfully forced one. "Hey." My voice cracks on that simple little word. I need to do a better job hiding my stupid emotions.

"Well, boys," Deena says, coming up behind me. She puts her arm over my shoulders. "Nice to see you both, but we've gotta go get ready."

Ready? *For what?*

"Ready?" Lucky asks. "For what?"

Deena gives the guys her best smile. "Double date." I turn my head slowly until we're making eye contact. I want to stop her, but there's no way.

"You." Joe points at me. "Who'd go out with *you?*" The jerk chuckles.

Deena makes a growly sound but only loud enough for me. "This girl," she pulls me to her side, "has lots of offers." She glares at my brother.

"No way." Joe shakes his stupid head.

For a brief second, I want to agree with my brother, but it hits me. Joe doesn't think I'm good enough to get asked out. And that belief hurts more than—than even last Friday night. The tears are sudden. Probably because my emotions are just right there on the surface. They've been hovering there for a week, and now they're out for all to see, which makes me cry harder.

"Becklyn?" Lucky sounds concerned.

Yeah. Right.

I see him move closer in my peripheral vision. Holding my hand up to stop him, I shake my head, which seems to work. He stops.

Looking at my brother, I ask what I should have asked him a long time ago. "Y-you have never thought I was good enough for anybody. Have you?"

The smile on Joe's face drops suddenly. "Becks…"

"You don't think anyone would ever want m-me."

"No." He's shaking his head. "Becks. That's not…"

I don't want to hear it. Now that I'm crying, which he hates, and I'm calling him out, which he hates even more, he's going to try to appease me. It's how Joe operates.

Well, I'm not going to let him pacify me this time. He can't just brush over this like his words didn't hurt.

Stepping away from all three of them, I pick up the pace and practically jog out of the gym. In the parking lot, I hear footsteps behind me. Assuming it's Deena, I slow down and turn back. I'm about to ask her to unlock her car when I see who's actually behind me.

Stopping suddenly, I look around the parking lot. For an escape route? Maybe.

Why can't I remember where we parked? Sometimes, I'm the biggest idiot.

"Becklyn."

"No." I shake my head. "I don't want your pity. Just leave me alone, Lucky."

The man never listens. Not to me, anyway, because by the time I find Deena's car, he's right beside me, repeating, "Becklyn."

I turn to face him and snap, "What, Lucky?"

"Your brother didn't mean that."

A glare is the best I can muster. The good thing about it is, I'm angry now so the tears have abated. "Yeah, he did."

Lucky shakes his head. "No. He didn't. Joe thinks you're—"

I hold up my hand for the second time in five minutes; it does its job. Lucky stops talking. "Don't explain my brother to me. He means it."

Lucky moves closer. One of his hands moves up. I watch as he gently touches my face. "Baby girl. No."

Baby girl? What the ever-loving heck?

"He didn't mean it."

My mouth opens, then closes without emitting a sound, because I'm still trying to figure out the "baby girl" thing. Also, the hand on my face thing. I clear my throat and try again. "Please don't apologize for him."

"Then, I'll apologize for me."

This is getting interesting.

"I'm sorry about Friday."

Suddenly, my mouth feels as dry as the Sahara. Swallowing is impossible. I try anyway.

"As I was leaving the house, Joe asked me where I was going." Lucky's eyes look sort of sad. "I had to tell him."

Why is he explaining this to me? It wasn't a date.

"When he heard we were gonna eat, he asked if he could go. Then, at your dorm, he jumped out of the car to run up to your room before I could stop him."

Sounds like Joe.

Lucky's stopped talking now. I guess I'm supposed to say something. "It's okay. I understand." Those two tiny sentences are both lies. I'm not okay, and I don't really understand because I'm an idiot. Lucky isn't to blame for anything to do with Friday night. It was all on me. I believed something that was just not possible. My fantasy world took over and left me with… nothing, I guess. I need to stop living in that world, pull my head out of the clouds, and face the fact that Joe is actually right. Nobody wants to date me. Deena made up the double date story to make Lucky jealous. It's obvious that didn't work.

Lucky's still got his hand there. His thumb is doing this weird thing running back and forth over my cheek. His fingers are resting on the back of my neck. It's forcing my attention up. "Who's the guy?"

Huh? "What guy?"

"Your date. Who's the guy?"

The frown on my face has to be obvious. "He's… nobody…"

"You ready, Becks?" Deena says, stepping up beside me. "We need to get going if we're ever going to be ready in time."

Shaking my head causes Lucky's hand to drop to his side. I miss it. "Deena, I—"

"Chop-chop, Becklyn." Deena pulls open the passenger door and holds it for me.

I know what she's doing, and it's pointless, but there's no way I'm getting into it right now. She's probably right to leave with him thinking I've got a date. At least if he assumes it's true, I don't leave here as pathetic. Turning, I look back at Lucky before I get in. "I guess I'll see you."

"You will."

What the heck is that supposed to mean?

No. Becklyn. Stop it. All he meant was I'd see him again. Of course I will. He's Joe's best friend.

13

BECKLYN

THE KNOCK ON THE DOOR GIVES ME PAUSE. I GLANCE OVER AT Deena, who's looking through her closet for the "perfect" outfit. Apparently, we are, in fact, going out tonight. I didn't bother fighting her on it. It seems like a good way to forget about everything. "I'll get it," she says, pulling out a little black dress.

I return to my flat iron, attempting to get my naturally curly hair to settle down. As the wand is sliding down, I hear her. "What the hell do you want?"

Wow. I've never heard her answer the door like that. Turning, I'm shocked to see Joe and Lucky at the door. I drop the hot hair tool, burning my hand, then my leg, since all I'm wearing is a short robe. "Ouch," I hiss.

"What happened?" Lucky pushes Joe out of his way and marches over to me. "You okay?"

I've got my finger in my mouth, sucking on it to get the pain to ebb. All I can do is nod.

"Babe," he says softly, kneeling in front of me. "Let me see."

Unable to process any of what he just said, I slide my finger out of my mouth slowly and hold it in front of him, reassuring him by saying, "It's okay."

79

He takes my hand in his and leans in closer. "You really burned it."

"It happens all the time. Getting all dolled up can be painful." I snicker.

"You need to be careful." He looks down at my leg. "You burned your leg?" His hand is on top of my thigh before I can protest. His big, long, warm fingers are gently tracing around the spot and I've gotta tell ya, I don't hate it.

"Jesus, Becks," my brother snaps from the doorway. "Put some damn clothes on."

"I—"

Deena beats me to the punch. "You barge into *our* home and think you can tell us what to do?" She's got her hands on her hips, her foot jutted out, and the tapping has commenced. "Get over yourself, asshole."

"This is none of your business." Joe's leaning in and bending a little bit so that he and Deena are inches apart. "Stay out of it."

"She *is* my business. You make her cry every time you see her."

"No." Joe shakes his head. "That's not true." He looks over at me. When our eyes meet, he blinks. "Right, Becks?"

I'm about to get up so I can move closer to him when I feel a palm full on my thigh. Heck, one of his fingers has found its way under the hem of my robe.

"Becklyn?" He's practically whispering.

So I whisper right back. "What?"

"Who are you going out with?"

"I told you. Nobody."

"So, I wouldn't know him?"

This is messing with my head. Why does he care? I go with the easiest answer. "No."

"Where's he taking you?"

There is no "he," but I sort of like the fact that Lucky is interested in my plans for tonight. "I think we're going to Illini Inn." Illini Inn is probably the most popular place for U of I college kids to hang out. And because they serve food, minors are allowed.

Lucky's expression morphs into one filled with concern. "You run into any problems, you call me, yeah?"

"Sure." The two of us are so close now I can see the flecks of gold in his eyes. God, he's beautiful. "But there won't be any problems." Because none of this is true. We'll probably go to the inn, Deena will meet someone, and I'll head home. It's how it works with the two of us.

"No matter. Call me if you need me."

"Sure, Lucky." I nod. Why argue with the guy?

With a little squeeze on my thigh, Lucky stands. That's when I realize the room has gone completely silent. When the two of us turn, both Joe and Deena are watching us. "What?" I ask, furrowing my brow.

"Nothing." Deena's smirk is obvious.

Joe's expression is unreadable.

"Well, see you boys later." Deena holds the door open and waves her arm to get them out. Once they're gone and the door is shut, she squeals like she just won the lottery. "Oh. My. God." She's now jumping up and down, clapping. "Lucky's so in love with you."

Here we go again. "No." I shake my head. "He's not, so please just stop right there. I can't go through another week of thinking he likes me when he doesn't. Let's just go out so you can land a guy." And I can come back and… sit here alone.

Deena crosses her arms in her usually defiant stance. "Did you happen to tell him where we're going?"

"Well, yeah. He asked—"

Uncrossing her arms, she steps over to me. Bending at the waist, she's as close to me as Lucky was a minute ago. "I'll bet you a night alone in the room he—"

Shaking that off, I refuse the bet. "No. You aren't getting me to fall for that again."

"Fine. I'll bet you a week of only listening to your crap music that Lucky will show up tonight." Crap music? Who is she kidding? My music rocks. Well, it's Country, but you get the gist.

"You're wrong." I know he won't show up, because he just told me to call him if I needed him. Which I won't, so I won't.

"We'll see." She stands upright and touches the top of my head. "Now. Let's get you looking hot as hell."

Whatever. I want to roll my eyes, because that's what she always says, and it never works.

"Wow, this place is dead."

I look around the Illini Inn and shrug. It's not dead, per se. I've only been here one other time after a big football win, and if she's basing it on that, then, yes, it's dead. "It'll probably pick up later."

"Hope you're right." She scans the bar. "Slim pickin's right now."

What she means is, there don't seem to be many men about. I'm not unhappy about that. Maybe the two of us will actually spend some time together. "Let's grab that booth." I point to the lone empty booth close to the back of the place.

"Score," she shouts. "At least we'll get a table."

We slide into a booth that has seen better days. The orange vinyl seat is cracked and worn. If this booth could talk, it'd probably have some good stories to tell. Heck, the entire bar is like that. "Dive bar" is what Joe always calls it. I'd call it casual and unpretentious. How can a place with dingy brown paneling on the walls and ancient lighted beer signs be pretentious? It can't. I settle into my seat and I'm about to ask Deena about her classes when the waitress stops by to get our order. While we wait, Deena does what she always does: she hunts her next prey.

"Got him." She smirks.

"Where?" I look to my right.

"Guy playing pool. Gray tee."

They're all wearing gray tees. "Ah. Yes." I have no idea who she's talking about, and I don't really want to know.

The second our drinks are placed in front of us, she's gone.

14

BECKLYN

"Hey, beautiful."

Okay, maybe she succeeded tonight, because for some reason, I've had several guys approach me. Not really knowing how to respond to this latest guy, I merely smile.

He holds his hand out and says, "I'm Chasen."

I place my hand in his. "Becklyn."

With my hand still in his, I watch as Chasen's eyes move from my face down to my chest. I know why he's doing that too. Deena chose a shirt I've never worn without a cami. To say I'm showing some skin is an understatement. It's embarrassing. In an attempt to draw his attention away from my boobage, I ask, "You go to school here?"

"I do." With my free hand, I tug my top up a little higher. Since my other hand is still in his, I tug on that too so I can get my hand back. In order to make it not seem rude, I pull free and reach for my glass of lemon-lime soda "with a twist." It's what Deena told me to get so it looks like I'm drinking alcohol. She says we'll "look more legit" that way.

I'm not sure I agree, but I found out a long time ago it was easier to just go with Deena's ideas—at least in these unfamiliar situations.

"What's your major?"

Another tip she gave me: "Never tell a guy your real major, Becks. They'll think you're too smart."

That's one suggestion I tend to ignore. Who wants a guy who can't stand a little intellectual competition? In this case, though, I go ahead and answer, "Undecided." It's not technically a lie. I don't know what I want to do yet. I'm pretty certain it isn't anything to do with renewable energy. Anyway, the second part of this little scheme requires a giggle. I do it. And it hurts deep in my soul. But I do it. "What about you?"

"Sports management." Then he winks. "I'm on the golf team."

"Golf? Are you any good?" Look at me, engaging in conversation. Go me!

"The best." He winks again, and I realize that's a thing. Winking.

"I've never played golf before."

"Maybe I should take you sometime."

"I don't have clubs."

"Oh…" He smirks. "I've got a *club* for you."

And right there. That's when I know that Chasen is not for me, because the guy just referred to his man part as a "club." I stare at him, waiting for a wink, but he disappoints.

In a ploy to end this thing right this minute, I giggle again, then look back over my shoulder. "Uh-oh. I think I'd better rescue my friend over there." I point behind me. It's a ruse, because I know for a fact that Deena Summers does not need rescuing.

"Stay." He reaches out and places his hand over my wrist. "Let's get to know each other."

Shaking my head, I attempt to get my hand out from beneath his, but he's got a good grip. "I need to go. She's—"

"She's fine." How the heck does he know? "We clocked the two of you when you walked in. She's with a buddy of mine."

"Oh." Crap.

He leans in so close, I pull back out of fear he'll try to kiss me or something. No thanks. "The minute you walked into the place; I knew I had to fuck you."

"Oh." The blush on my face has to be florescent pink. Who says that to a stranger anyway?

"Does that surprise you?"

"Yes."

"I understand." He smirks. "Not many guys like big girls, but I…."

I refuse to listen to the rest of that sentence. I've heard enough —for a lifetime. Attempting to yank my hand out from beneath his once again, I'm about to ask him to let me out of the booth when we're interrupted by someone other than Deena sliding into the seat across from us.

Of course it is. It's Lucky Ganetti.

"Hey." He grunts the single-syllable word and gives Chasen a chin lift. Then he looks at me. "How are you?"

"I'm—"

I don't get a chance to finish, because the one and only Tiff appears. "Where'd you go, Lucky?" Her eyes move around the booth. The second she spots me, she frowns. Then her eyes move to Chasen. "Chasen. What on earth are you doing?"

"I'm talking to my new friend, Becky."

"Becklyn," Lucky and I say at the exact same time.

Chasen shrugs.

"Why?" Tiffany looks quite confused. Her extra, extra-long fake eyelashes are fluttering so fast, I swear I can feel the breeze she's generating.

"Why am I talking to Becky, here?"

"Becklyn." It's just me this time.

Tiffany's expression is confused but also something more

sinister. Crossing her arms over her chest, I can't help noticing how much her boobs move up. They're practically popping out of her low-cut top. "Is this one of your stupid bets?"

A bet?

Looking back at me, she explains, "They do it *all* the time." She rolls her eyes. "They pick the ugl—" She covers her mouth. "I mean… they choose a girl who's not…" She pauses again and points at me. "Girls like you." She smiles because she probably thinks she's found the best way to insult me.

She did.

"Anyhoo, they bet to see how long it takes them to talk her into doing them in the back room."

I hear a growl coming from the other side of the table, but I can't think about Lucky right now. All I can think about is this predicament I'm in.

This is a humiliating, embarrassing, and anger-inducing predicament.

The last thing I wanted was for Lucky to hear any of that. For him to hear what guys really think of me.

Tiffany's still yapping. She's now talking to Chasen. "I'm right, aren't I? It's a bet." She looks over her shoulder at the table where Deena is sitting with three other guys. "You have to stop doing that. It's *so* rude." She looks at me, and all I see is pity on her face. Her brows have been pushed together, and she's got puckered lips.

Oh, I'm not going to like this. Not one bit.

She bends forward a little. "Honey," she says so sugar-sweetly but also condescendingly. "You can't really think that a guy like Chasen would be interested in *you*, do you?"

"I—" Truthfully, I don't care. I don't want him to be interested in me. The guy's a jerk.

"He's the president of the Teke fraternity. He'd *never* date someone like you."

In times like these, the threat of tears is usually imminent.

But do you want to know something? I'm not going to cry this time, because I'm not sad. *I'm pissed.* Who do these people think they are? I look over at Lucky, and I can't decide if I should be happy or mad. He looks like he wants to kill Chasen. He's glaring at the guy with his hands in fists on top of the table. If you ask me, he should be glaring at her. Tiffany. She's the one saying all the mean stuff. Who cares about the jerk golfer guy? Not me.

Turning my head, I say to Chasen, the dick, "Please move."

"Huh?" He's finally noticed me.

His complete attention has been on Tiffany, but he's looking at me now. "Let. Me. Out."

"Oh. Right." He slides out of the booth. Once I'm out, he slides back in, and Tiff moves in next to Lucky.

I turn to leave but think better of it. How many times in my life have I just let people talk to me like that?

A million and one. That's how many. And every time it happens, I walk away and think of a million and two things I should have said in rebuttal. Then I usually cry.

Not this time.

Nope. This time, I'm going to say my piece. (*Then*, I'll cry.)

Looking down at Chasen, I say, "You're a dick. And don't ever call your penis a 'club' again—that's just gross."

Tiffany giggles.

I turn to her. "And I have no idea what your problem is, Tiff, but I just feel sorry for you."

Suddenly, she's the one that looks affronted.

She shouldn't be shocked. It's the truth. Why does someone as pretty as her need to put other women down? She's seemingly got it all.

She has Lucky, for crying out loud.

My eyes go to Lucky next. He's no longer glaring at Chasen. He's looking right at me. We stare at one another for several seconds. I'm not sure what I'm waiting for. Perhaps I'd like to see him push Tiff onto the floor and wrap me up in his arms and kiss me.

Instead, I get nothing.

With that knowledge, I turn and stomp through the crowd and out the front door. The more I stomp, the angrier I get.

Which is pretty darned angry. I'm Irish, after all.

I make it down to the end of the street to the corner, and just as I'm about to turn left, I hear my name. I know who it is instantly, so I pick up the pace. He had his chance to say something back at the inn, but he didn't say a word.

"Becklyn. Wait."

I don't. Instead, I stomp double time.

"Come on, Becklyn."

He's getting closer, thanks to his stupidly long legs. Heck, he's probably not even trying that hard. I feel his hand wrap around my upper arm. I whip around to face him, hoping it dislodges his hand. It does. "What do you want?"

"I just wanted to make sure you're okay."

Crossing my arms in front of me, I can't help noticing his eyes flick down to my top. Ignoring that, I answer in as bitchy a tone as I can muster, "I'm fine. Perfect, actually. Couldn't be better. Thanks for asking." I raise my hand and point in the direction we both just came. "Now, go back to your mean girl girlfriend."

"Becklyn," Lucky growls.

No. *He* doesn't get to sound angry.

I do.

With my own growl, I turn away from Lucky and just as I'm about to march, his hand wraps around my upper arm again. "Becklyn, wait."

"What!" I spin so fast I nearly lose my balance. The only thing that saves me is Lucky. He reaches out and ends up with one hand on each of my shoulders to stop my momentum. "Just..." I don't even know what to say. I certainly don't want to recap what just happened at the bar. Remembering it suddenly overwhelms my emotions. I'm so sick of people and their ability to bring me to my proverbial knees with their stupid, ugly words. I know I won't be able to hide my emotions, not from him. So, I don't bother. I feel the tears just on the surface, but I fight them off. "Lucky, I just want to be alone."

"Baby girl…"

Why does he keep calling me that?

"No." I shake my head. "I want to go home."

"Becklyn." Lucky's voice is but a whisper.

So is mine. "Lucky."

"Let me drive you. I don't want you walking alone."

"I walk all over the place alone."

"Please. Let me drive you."

It's probably no use arguing with him. He seems particularly domineering tonight. "Fine."

I get a small smile out of him. I guess that's nice. "You wait right here. I'll get the car."

Giving him my sweetest smile, I answer, "Sure."

Lucky's right hand rises, his pointer finger aimed right at me. "Don't move."

"Nope." I shake my head like I mean it.

Lucky turns and starts to jog back in the direction of the bar. As soon as he's a half block away, I take the opportunity to make a run for it.

For some reason, the whole notion of me attempting to get home before he can catch me causes a giggle to start in my chest and burst from my lips. By the time I've rounded the next block, I'm laughing my butt off. I see headlights turn onto the street. It's got to be him. With a maneuver that can only be described as genius, I take a right onto a sidewalk that takes me between two campus buildings. "Ha. Let's see you get your car through here, Lucky Ganetti."

Still giggling, I wave as I pass a few people walking in the opposite direction. They probably either think I'm drunk or crazy. Maybe both. As soon as I pass through the buildings, I'm on a street secluded by trees. From here, I can see my building. I don't see Lucky anywhere, but now isn't the time to become complacent. Using the trees as cover, I make my way slowly toward my dorm. I've only got one more street to cross and I'll be home free. Looking right, then left to ensure there's no traffic coming, I race across the street. Panting, I make my way to the front door of my building. Reaching into my back pocket for my key card, I'm shocked when someone grasps my shoulders, turns me around quickly, and presses me up against the glass door.

"You. Are a brat, Foxy." Lucky's panting too.

A fresh set of giggles erupts. It can't be helped.

"I told you to wait for me."

"I didn't want to."

"Like I said. Brat."

I should be mad at him using that word, but I'm not. It was really bratty of me to take off. Heck, it wasn't like he should be surprised. I shrug. "Sorry."

Lucky moves in. That's when I realize just how close he is and that my back is up against the door. His hands that were on my shoulders have slowly made their way down my arms. Then, one of them moves up. He touches my face again, like he did that one other time. I feel his fingers slide into my hair, and while I should worry about the fact I'm extremely sweaty, I can't. I'm too busy trying to remember how to breathe, because he's moving closer. And closer. And closer.

When he's a half inch away, he whispers, "Brat." Which makes me smile. A smile that drops the second I realize that Lucky Ganetti is kissing me. *Me*. Becklyn Morrissey.

His lips are soft. The kiss is gentle. And slow. I get the distinct feeling I need to let Lucky take the lead. Since I really have no idea what to do anyway, that's A-OK with me. I mean, my only real experience kissing happened at Y-camp in seventh grade. His name was Lloyd. After the kiss, he proceeded to tell everyone that I was "experienced."

Not good, because in seventh grade Y-camp terms, he was telling everyone I was a hussy. Ridiculous, since the only kissing I'd even seen was on television. Soap operas in particular.

I never spoke to Lloyd again.

Good thing he lived in a town far, far away from mine. I would have hated to get a reputation.

When Lucky presses closer to me, I feel his other hand wrap around my back. Since I want to do something, I raise my arms and wrap them around his neck, pulling him even closer. His groan causes chills to run over my entire body. My nipples especially. His tongue enters my mouth, and my instinct tells me I need to do the same. When my tongue touches his, Lucky's soft, sweet kiss suddenly turns into something else. Something more.

He presses closer, if that's possible. He turns his head enough for his mouth to take mine in a heated, open-mouthed, passionate kiss. I'm sort of overwhelmed with it. I can't ignore his palm on my butt. I squeak when he squeezes one of my cheeks. Lucky's mouth moves from mine to my cheek, then down the side of my neck. He sounds breathless as he says "Foxy" in my ear.

"Lucky," I say back.

I'm not sure if that's the thing that did it, the thing that ruined it, but at my utterance of his name, he suddenly pulls away. His hands go up to my shoulders as he steps back, essentially pushing me away.

Running a hand through his hair, he mutters, "Fuck."

"Lucky?" I reach out toward him, but he moves away from me, taking several steps back.

Shaking his head, he won't look at me. "I'm sorry, Becklyn. That never should have happened. It was a mistake."

"Oh."

A mistake.

Of course it was.

I mean… why would Lucky Ganetti want to kiss *me*?

"Right." I reach into my pocket, grasp my key card, slide it through the reader, and I'm inside my building before he has a chance to make me feel worse.

Like that's possible.

I don't bother looking back, because no way do I want to see his face.

By the time I get to my room, I've convinced myself that what just happened wasn't a big deal. Because like Lucky said, it was a mistake.

Stripping out of my clothes, I roll them into a ball and toss them in my hamper. Searching my room for some pj's, I find my trusty old onesie. I'm sliding them up my legs when my phone chimes.

"Crap." I forgot to tell Deena I was leaving. It's probably her.

Zipping myself in, I search for my phone and realize it's still in my jeans. The second I locate it, the name on the screen surprises me.

Lucky: Please don't tell Joe.

I blink at the screen, thinking. Then, I reply.

Me: I will never speak of it.

To anyone.

Not even Deena.

Why would I embarrass myself further? As for him? He just got caught up in the moment. That's all. No reason to embarrass him either.

I quickly send Deena a message letting her know I am back in the dorm. She responds soon after with just "K." Sliding into my bed, I do my level best not to remember it. The kiss. Because the best thing I can do for myself is to forget it. To forget about Lucky Ganetti and move on with my life.

And that's exactly what I intend to do. Even if it kills me.

15

BECKLYN

Fall

"New year, new digs, new major for you... new *everything*," Deena says as she practically dances around our home away from home. We're in the process of moving into our new apartment. The one we rented after deciding dorm life sucked. It turns out renting an apartment is cheaper than living in the dorms. Mind you, our place is a tiny two-bedroom. Not as small as our dorm, and like I said, it has two bedrooms. Which means I will no longer have to find somewhere else to sleep when Deena decides to bring someone home.

But that may be over, because Deena met someone over the summer. He's a student here. I haven't met him yet, but she says he's "amazing."

I'll have to take her word for it. Honestly, as long as she's happy, I'm happy.

"Too bad your brother isn't around to help us lug up the sofa."

"Uh-huh." I'm not sad about it. I was ready for Joe to move on with his life so I can live mine. Does that make me sound like a terrible sister?

It's all good. Joe landed his dream job in San Francisco. The one he had interviewed for that time I slept in his room. Mom freaked out on him when she found out, but when he explained to her that he loved the company and the idea of living somewhere exciting, well, how could she be upset?

It was time for Joe to fly the nest. For him to spread his wings and maybe grow up.

"What's Lucky up to?"

I do my best not to let her see my eyes roll. She knows something happened between the two of us, but I never told her the story. All I said was he didn't defend me when Tiffany was mean-girling me.

It worked, because after that, whenever she even heard the word "lucky," she'd make a hissing sound.

"I've no idea." That's no lie. I haven't seen Lucky since that night. The one when he kissed me. After, I did my utter best to avoid anything Lucky-related. Even at Joe's graduation party, I was able to make a brief appearance and then leave. Joe was so wasted, he didn't even notice.

Since then, I spent my summer working at our hometown grocery store. At first, I was concerned I'd see him now and then, but I'd heard early on that he was in Chicago for the summer doing some sort of physical therapy internship. As far as I know, that company could have hired him. He didn't come home over the summer. At least, I never saw him. I sort of felt sorry for his dad, but it made things easier for me.

"Do you think you'll see him this semester?"

Crap. She's still talking about Lucky.

"I doubt it." He no longer lives with my brother, of course. They had to move out of their little rental house when Joe graduated. "I don't have a clue where he is. He graduated." I shrug.

"Hm." Deena's voice sounds a bit strange.

"Why? What do you know?"

"Maybe…"

With a sigh, I set down the box of dishes my mom scrounged up for us. "Spill."

"He lives here." She titters. "In this same complex."

"No." She cannot be serious.

"Yes."

"How do you know?"

"I was heading into the management office and he was coming out."

Slapping my forehead with my palm, I make a groaning noise. "So he knows I'm here?"

Shaking her head, she snickers. "He didn't see me. I hid behind a bush."

Thank goodness.

"But I followed him."

I gasp. What if he saw her?

"Relax." She waves me off. "I was super sleuthy. He didn't see me. He lives in building five."

We're in two. "Great," I mutter sarcastically. "I'm sure we'll run into each other at some point." How could we not?

"Well, you've done your best to avoid him. You quit hanging out with your brother. Going to the ass-crack of dawn kickboxing classes our last five weeks last spring ensured you wouldn't see him at the gym."

She's right. Somehow, I found the will to get up at four thirty in the morning just to make it to the 5:00 AM kickboxing class.

"You look good, by the way."

I smile at my best friend. "Thanks." I didn't stop working out when I went home over the summer. I found a regular kickboxing class at a nearby Y that enabled me to keep up with the workout. I love kickboxing. I'm pretty good at it too.

"How much weight did you lose, anyway?"

"Hardly any."

"No way."

I snicker. "Way." Apparently, muscle weighs more than fat, and I've definitely gained muscle. "I've just firmed up." I slap my own thigh.

"Your body is h-a-w-t." She nods approvingly. "Not only that, but you're wearing clothes that actually fit. Thank fuck. I was getting really sick of those giant T-shirts and sweatshirts."

"Hey," I protest. "I still love those." I still work out in those clothes. But she's right. I'm feeling a lot more confident in my own skin now, which seems to translate into me choosing new clothes that don't hang on me.

"Well, the minute Lucky gets a look at the new you, he's gonna flip."

"He's not."

"I'll bet you—"

"No." I release a startled laugh. "No bets." Not about Lucky, anyway. That's over. Done. Like Deena just said, new year, new life, new house, oh, and new major. I've done a complete one-eighty, as they say, as regards to my degree. After some soul searching and good talks with my parents, I've decided to change my major to… drum roll please… education. I'm going to be a teacher. A high school science teacher, to be exact.

My dad has always loved his job. He whistles first thing in the morning and everything. Plus, he gets his summers off. There's something really appealing about that as well. When I told him I was thinking about a degree in education, he was beyond thrilled.

"A chop off the ol' Billy block," he'd said.

I guess he's right.

16

BECKLYN

It takes nearly two weeks before I see him. And before he sees me. Hopping off the bus at the stop right by our apartment complex, I make my way toward my building and see movement to my left, causing me to glance that way. I recognize his car first. A dark blue Ford Mustang that he's had since high school. Lucky is busy doing something under his hood. Even though I can't see his face, I'd know that body anywhere.

He looks good.

Stepping closer, I hear him mumbling things to himself.

"Car trouble?" I ask in as cheery a voice as I can muster even though I'm a nervous wreck. It's been months since I've seen him. *Months.* While I should probably keep my mouth shut, the truth is, I've missed him. Besides, I can't just pass by him without acknowledging him.

Startled, Lucky bumps his head on his car hood causing me to wince for him. "You okay?"

He turns his head slowly. When our eyes meet, I suck in a lungful of air and hold it.

God, he's gorgeous.

"Becklyn?" Lucky says, sounding surprised. "Are you looking

99

for me?" His voice changed just then, to something rather hopeful.

"No." I point toward building two. "I live here."

He looks to where I'm pointing. "You do?"

"I do." I force a look on my face that hopefully shows confusion. "Why are you here? Did you come to see *me?*"

Ha. See what I did there?

"I live here too. Five."

"Oh."

"You look different."

I feel different.

"I do?"

"Your hair." Lucky steps closer and reaches out to touch my hair but stops before he gets there. "You cut it."

"I did." And boy, was that a tough decision. I've had long hair my entire life, but one day this summer, I'd had an epiphany. The hair stylist called it a "sleek bob," but that look only happens if I take the time to use the flat iron on it, which I don't on most days. Days like today. So, mine is more of a messy bob. No matter, I love it. There's just something about the act of changing one's hair that gives us a new outlook on life. Plus, it's liberating.

"It's so curly." Lucky seems mesmerized by my hair. I'd laugh if I weren't a little mesmerized myself.

"I guess cutting off ten inches of hair will do that."

"You look…"

I hold my breath because I'm a little afraid of what he's going to say.

"Older."

Could've been worse, I guess.

"Thanks?" I laugh a little.

Lucky smiles as he reaches out again and touches one of the curls next to my cheek. He pulls on it gently, then releases it, causing it to bounce back into place, sort of. "Beautiful."

The pair of us stand in silence. Painful silence, honestly. I decide to end it before something bad happens. "Welp," I say, clapping my hands once. "This homework isn't going to do itself."

"Joe mentioned you changed your major."

Not a surprise that he's talked to Joe. They're best friends, after all.

"Yep. Secondary science education."

"A teacher, huh?"

Shrugging, I adjust my slipping backpack. "Just like dear old dad."

"I can see you teaching."

That's a nice thing to say.

Sort of absently, Lucky says, "You'll have all the high school guys drooling over you."

Shock. That's why my mouth drops open and my eyes bug out. "Excuse me?"

Lucky must realize what he said was a bit strange. Is he blushing? "Sorry."

A nervous laugh shoots out of my mouth. "Don't be." It's a compliment, I suppose.

"You been at the gym? Smiths?" He gestures at my outfit. I'm wearing some workout gear. Actually, it's the stuff I bought to go on my non-date with him.

"Uh, sort of." I'm not sure if I should tell him. I guess it wouldn't hurt. "I got a job there."

"A job?" We make eye contact. "Doing what?"

"Teaching the 5:00 AM kickboxing class." It was a shock to me too.

I guess all my effort over the summer really paid off, because the first class back at Smith's Gym, the tyrannical little instructor approached me about taking over the class. At first, I thought she was joking, but she said, "You've come a long way, girl. I won't be able to teach this timeslot anymore due to my full-time job. They've been looking for someone for a while. If you're interested, head to the office for information. Tell them I sent you."

I don't know why, but I did it. I went to the office and asked. They had me go through three classes that constituted teacher training, and after those, I had the job. Answering Lucky, I smile. "Starting tomorrow, I'm the new kickboxing instructor for that early class."

"Holy shit, Becklyn." His smile is wide and sincere. I can tell. When he wraps his arms around me and draws me into a hug, I have to hold my breath. He still makes me feel all fluttery when he touches me. "That's amazing. Congratulations."

With my face pressed into his chest, I'm torn between saying "Thanks" and just sniffing him. Of course, I go with the former, but I get a little of the latter in there too.

I'm clever like that.

Reluctantly, I pull away and take a step back. "I'm nervous."

"Babe," Lucky says softly. Bending down so we're eye to eye, he adds, "You're going to be amazing."

I hate it when he calls me babe, because I know it doesn't mean anything, but I really wish it did.

"Well, I don't know about that."

"Hey, Morrissey."

I quickly turn to see who just said that. Oh, it's just my annoying neighbor. The same guy who plays video games online all night long. Loudly. "Oh, hey, Matt."

"Lookin' good, Becks." He points and winks.

Turning back to Lucky, I roll my eyes.

In a deep, rather angry voice, Lucky asks, "Who was he?"

"Neighbor."

"Oh, yeah? You hang out with him?"

"Sometimes." We've had them over for pizza, and they've had us over to watch a game. "They live next door."

"I don't like him." Lucky's still glaring at the front door to building number two. "You should probably stay away from that guy."

Weird. "Sure, Lucky." I smile because I'm not sure what else to do. "Well, I'd better get going. I really do have a paper to write."

"Sure," Lucky says with a weak smile. "See you soon, Becklyn."

Wow, that almost sounded like a threat.

A threat I'd welcome, to be honest.

What?

Oh, I know what you're thinking, but all I can say is, a girl doesn't get over her first love so easily. At least not this girl.

Still, I need to remember everything that went down last spring and how it all made me feel. Recalling it may make me stronger. At least strong enough not to get caught up in Lucky again.

17

LUCKY

I'M IN TROUBLE.

I stayed away from her all summer. Hell, since last April. Kissing her was the worst idea I've ever had, because once I got a taste of her, I didn't want to stop.

And now, here she is with that curvy little bod in her tight jeans and fitted top with the sexiest fucking hair I've ever seen. All I want to do is throw her over my shoulder and take her to my bed. I want to kiss, touch, and lick every fucking inch of her. And after we're done, I want to wrap every little ringlet of hair around my fingers just to feel the softness and watch them spring back into place.

Jesus. Her face.

So. Fucking. Beautiful.

I'm so screwed.

Joe's gonna kill me, but I can't wait any longer. I've put off the inevitable for too long. For him. For our friendship. He's been my best friend since I moved down the street from the Morrisseys. Hell, Mrs. M. and Billy are like parents to me. Honestly, I have no idea how they'd react to the news I've had a thing for their youngest child for as long as I can remember.

No matter. Joe's just going to have to get over it. He's going to have to accept the fact that his baby sister has been mine for a long, long time. I knew it the night of her junior prom....

I was home from college to help my dad with something. When I stopped over to the Morrisseys', Joe told me he was upset for his sister. That it was her prom, and she wasn't going.

Told you he loved his little sister.

I didn't think much of it. I figured it was because she just didn't want to go, but Joe told me that no one had asked her. To say I was shocked is an understatement, because she was such a cool girl even back then. Funny, smart, and goddamn beautiful.

That revelation hit me like a ton of bricks.

Not only that, Becklyn didn't seem the least bit sad about missing her junior prom. Instead, she made plans for a movie night with her mom and dad. She made popcorn and wore the most ridiculous pajamas I'd ever seen. It was one of those one-piece things that zip up in the front—hers had bunny ears and a tail. All I could think, at the time, was how fucking cute she was. And perfect.

That was it. That was the night I knew I was screwed. I've done my goddamn best to avoid her—done a good job too—until the night she showed up at the St. Paddy's Day party. At least that's the night I thought was my breaking point. Looking at her now, with her tousled hair and her sexy workout clothes, St. Patrick's Day was nothing. Because this new version of Becklyn Morrissey is dangerous.

She already has my heart.

Now I've got to win hers.

Me: Pick you up at 4:30

Risky move though it is, I can't stand the thought of her hopping on a city bus at four in the morning, alone. That time of night, there are crazies about. No, it's my duty as, well, as her friend to make sure she gets to Smith's safely. Besides, this gives me a chance to get my workout in, since my afternoons are packed with school shit.

No, this is a great idea.

The fact that I'll be able to observe her through the wall of glass windows is a bonus.

18

BECKLYN

I blink at the message on my phone. "He's not coming to my class. Is he?"

"He who?"

I glance at Deena, who's eating a bowl of my favorite cereal. "That's all you get of my cereal."

"Whatevs." She gives me her patented eye roll and shoves another spoonful in her mouth. With her mouth stuffed with Captain's Crunch, I'm able to make out the words, "I'll buy more."

Pulling up the keyboard, I'm about to reply when she asks again, "Who are you talking about?"

"Lucky."

The clink, clank of the spoon as it hits the counter draws my attention back to Deena. "Lucky?" she shrieks. "You talked to him? When? Where?"

I should've known this was going to happen. The girl is like a dog with a bone when she wants information. So, I set my phone down and tell her. "Outside. We chatted for a few minutes. I told him about my new job, and now he wants to pick me up and drive me in the morning."

"He's going to your class?" Deena's face is half shock, half glee. If that's even possible.

"He'd better not be." No way would I be able to teach with Lucky in the room. I'm already terrified for tomorrow, even though I have Kelsey's (the previous instructor) notebook with her workout routines listed out step-by-step. Even with those cheat sheets, if you will, I'm still super nervous. "I'll kill him," I mutter, but Deena still hears me.

"Incentive."

"Incentive? For what?" Sometimes….

"To do your best." She starts to play with her hair, and I start to worry. "Maybe I should come too, although I'm not a morning person," she arches one brow, "as you know."

"Oh, I know." Trust me. She's definitely not a morning person.

"So. What are you going to wear? You need to wear your cutest outfit."

Over the summer, I invested in some workout leggings and tops that match. For some reason, and Deena was right about this, when you feel like you look cute while working out, it's more fun. Honest to goodness. It's the truth.

Absently, I wave her off but say, "I'm wearing my new navy blue set." That will appease her. Picking my phone back up, I decide to nip this in the bud.

Me: Thanks anyway but I'm good.

Sure, a ride would've been nice but…
A second later, he replies.

Lucky: Picking you up at 4:30. Don't argue.

Okay. I'm just going to have to say it.
Here goes…

Me: Lucky, you cannot come to my very first class. I'm nervous as it is.
Lucky: I make you nervous?

I have to think about this question. It's a trick.

Me: No. You don't make me nervous…

Yes, he does.

Me: I'm nervous for my first day and I'd prefer my first class be complete strangers. Let me try this out a few times before you decide to pop in and critique me.
Lucky: Critique you? I wouldn't.
Me: Come on, Lucky… I'm going to be worried about what I'm doing as is. I'd prefer you didn't see the train wreck right away.
Lucky: I wasn't planning on going to your class. I was going to do my usual workout. It helps me since I haven't had time in the afternoon to get there. So, driving you gets me there too. This isn't about you.

Oh, well, that sort of stung.

Me: Fine. Thank you. I appreciate the gesture. See you at 4:30.
Lucky: Yep

"Morning," I mumble, sliding into Lucky's passenger seat—but since it's the first word out of my mouth this morning, it comes out sort of scratchy.

"Here." He hands me a travel cup. "Made you a smoothie."

I take the stainless-steel cup in hand and bring it to my nose to sniff. "Banana?"

"Among other things."

"I'm not sure I can eat yet." My stomach is literally flipping over. "Sort of feel nauseous."

"You're gonna be great. Just take a couple sips, see if it helps."

Placing the cup to my lips, I tip it back just enough to get about a teaspoon of the drink. "Mm. Good." And it is, but I'm still wary about eating or drinking anything just yet. Placing it in his cupholder, I glance over at him. I take a moment to check him out, because I don't think I've ever seen him this early in the day before.

He looks good. His hair looks like he styled it, but there's no way he'd shower before he goes to the gym, right? He's wearing a college tee and what looks to be a pair of sweatpants. I suspect he's got shorts on underneath the pants, along with some other things that I'm no longer allowed to fantasize about. It's none of my business what Lucky Ganetti has in his pants.

"What's with the notebook?"

"Kelsey's workouts."

"Kelsey?" He looks over at me. "She the instructor before you?"

"Yeah."

The car is silent for several minutes. Ordinarily, it wouldn't bother me, but today it does. "So, grad school, huh?"

I neglected to ask him about his reason for coming back to school this fall. The last I heard, he was going to work for the clinic in Chicago he interned at over the summer.

"Yeah," he says softly. "Changed my mind about a few things."

"Oh?" I hadn't heard about any of this. When I sent Joe a text asking him why Lucky was back, he told me he'd decided on grad school at the last minute. "What kind of changes?"

"We're here."

I look up and see the sign for Smith's Gym and remember why I'm here, and my stomach does a double flip. "I feel sick."

I feel his hand on my knee and a squeeze, and before I can even look down, it's gone. "You're going to be great."

How the heck does he know?

19

LUCKY

"WELL? HOW WAS IT?" IT'S A TRICK QUESTION. I WATCHED ALMOST her entire class thanks to the mirrors on the back wall of the gym. She kicked ass, and I mean that.

"I think it was okay." She's sweaty but smiling. "Everyone seemed to work up a sweat." She runs a hand through the front of her hair. "Even me."

"Did you enjoy it?"

"I did." Her smile is contagious. "I'm ready for that smoothie now."

When we slide into my car, I wait until she gets buckled in to hand her the smoothie she left in the cupholder. "Thanks." I watch her take a sip, then a bigger drink. Her throat bobs up and down, and for an instant, all I want to do is wrap her up in my arms and lick and kiss that neck.

But I can't. Not yet.

"Mm." Her voice sounds husky.

It's sexy as hell.

"This is delicious."

"I'm glad you like it. Lots of protein, and of course potassium, vitamins B6 and C."

115

"Nutritious." She gives me a small smile. I love her little smiles. Maybe even better than her big ones, because the little ones are intended for one person. In this case, it's me.

As we pull up to our apartment complex, I say, "Same time tomorrow." It's not a question.

I feel her hand on my forearm, and I nearly flinch. A jolt of something rushes up my arm. I've felt it before with her. Every time we touch, I feel it all through my body. "You don't need to drive me, Lucky."

"Told you. You're doing me a favor. Don't argue."

"Bossy," she mumbles as she reaches for the doorhandle.

"Guilty."

Sliding out of the seat, she reaches for the gym bag at her feet. "Thanks for the ride."

I'd like to give her a different ride.

"And for the smoothie."

"No problem, Becklyn. Have a good day, babe."

"You too."

I watch the door shut and then her ass as she makes her way up to her front door. That's when I realize that her ass, while always nice, is now fucking phenomenal. The combination of kickboxing and tight-as-sin workout clothes is both good and bad. Good because I get to see just how beautiful her body is. Bad, because so does every other asshole.

I growl, and the sound echoes through my car. The thought of someone else touching what's mine, well, that fucking pisses me off.

"Not gonna happen." At least not if I can prevent it.

It's been almost two weeks of driving my girl to work. Each morning, I wait outside her building in my car. When I see her silhouette appear, I smile, wondering what she's gonna be wearing. She doesn't seem to have a lot of variation to her workout gear, but no matter what she's wearing, she looks both adorable and hot as sin. Even this early in the morning, my dick wakes up at the sight of her.

I also prepare her a smoothie for the ride every day. I've made her several berry smoothies and one peanut butter concoction, but she always talks about the banana from the first day so I've been making her mostly those each morning.

She's not much of a talker at 4:30 AM, but by six, when her class is over, she's a damn chatterbox. She makes me laugh as she regales me with stories of the people who come to her class each morning. Actually, enrollment for the class has gone up quite a bit since she started. I guess word has gotten around that it's a tough workout, but she doesn't yell at anyone like Kelsey used to. Actually, the word I keep hearing about her teaching style is "encouraging."

Anyway, on the ride home, she tells me about this woman or that guy in her class and the things they do that make her laugh to herself. Like the guy who grunts when he does push-ups even though he's not really doing push-ups. He's mostly on all fours raising and lowering his upper body. "I've tried to show him proper technique. He does it right for a few reps but then goes right back to his old way."

"He's not getting any benefit from his way."

"Right?" she says as she sips her smoothie. "And don't get me started on his planks."

"I think I'll join your class tomorrow."

"No." She shakes her head. "No way."

"Why not?" I'm seriously asking. "You've had plenty of time to get used to it. Everybody leaves your class sweaty and tired. I need that."

"Lucky." Becklyn is whining.

"Becklyn." I give her my best annoyed side-eye. "I'm coming to your class. Get over it."

"Fine." She gives me her own version of the side-eye. "But, be prepared. I'm going to make you sweat."

Why does that statement make me think of sex? Oh, I know why….

"Challenge accepted."

Both of them.

2 0

———————

BECKLYN

I can't believe this. Deena is coming to my 5:00 AM class too. When I told her about Lucky's plan to join, she smiled. I certainly didn't expect to see her dressed and ready to go at four fifteen. She followed me downstairs and climbed into the back seat of Lucky's car, never uttering a word. So, here I am, ready to start class. A class that's packed to the gills. So much so, people have to share the freestanding punching bags. So, I've got that to worry about, plus I have both Lucky and Deena to contend with. I think the only thing I can do is make them work so hard, they won't pay a bit of attention to my actual teaching and maybe they won't come back.

Maybe.

"Alright, everybody. Let's warm up. Jab right." I demonstrate the jab motion and incorporate the movement of my hips from left to right. I do my best to explain what I'm doing for those who aren't quite awake this morning.

Deena.

"Good. Now, right jab, left cross."

The warmup with stretching takes about fifteen minutes. Honestly, it's a good workout on its own. Sweat has already

119

started to build up around my hairline. I make sure to warm up all body parts, especially the legs, since today's workout is really all about the lower body.

At five minutes left of class, I run through some stretches that focus on all the leg muscles we used kicking the bag, doing squats, and lots and lots of knee lifts. When it's all said and done, everyone is sweaty and exhausted.

My work is done.

"Wow," Deena says, looking like a soggy mess. "You're amazing."

Smiling, I give her ass a swat. "You did well this morning. You should come every—"

"No." She shakes her head as she wipes her face with her pink towel. "No way. Too early." Winking, she adds, "I'm glad I got to experience your class, though. Maybe they'll promote you to the afternoon session. If they do, I'll be there."

Shutting down the sound system, I search the area for my gloves and water bottle.

"Got it," Lucky says, holding up my bright blue bottle. Reaching for it, I place my hand on the bottle, but his doesn't budge, which means we're touching. "You"—he looks down at me as he steps closer—"are the best fucking instructor I've ever had."

No way. "No." I shake my head. I feel his finger touch my chin, forcing me to look at him.

"I'm not just saying that shit, Becklyn. Everybody's talking about how good your class is. That's you, babe. They're going to need to put you in the larger space soon."

I look around the room and frown. "It is pretty tight."

"They're going to need to invest in more bags too."

"Oh." I nod because I'm not sure what to say.

He taps my chin once, then his hand disappears. "Best fucking class, honey. Hands down."

Honey? Babe?

I wish he wouldn't use those terms, but if I say anything, he'll stop, and the alternative is far worse than that, because even if Lucky's terms of endearment are meant as merely friendly or brotherly, I'll take them.

Lucky takes my bag and throws it over his shoulder. The same as he does every morning. "I'm comin' back."

"Is that a threat?" I giggle.

"It's a promise."

I roll my eyes, but inwardly, I'm excited. I'm no longer going to worry about what Lucky thinks about my class, because he likes it. And, honestly, I know I'm pretty good. I've gotten a lot better, too, ever since I started creating my own workouts. Kelsey's book helped me get a rhythm, but I've put my own twist on things in an attempt to make it more fun. Plus, I do my best to inspire rather than berate. Positive reinforcement always works on me, so why not do it here?

As we leave the building, I look around for Deena. "She's already in the car. Gave her my keys."

"Right. She's tired."

"We all are. You're like the Tasmanian Devil in there."

I shrug because I'm not sure if that's a compliment or not.

I'm taking a drink of my water when he asks, "You wanna come over for dinner tonight? I'll make chicken piccata."

I nearly choke at his words. "Me?"

"Who else is here?" he chuckles.

I'm not sure how to answer him. I'd love to say yes, but, "I've, um, got something going on tonight."

"School stuff?" he asks, reaching for the passenger door handle.

"Date stuff."

Lucky stops moving. His hand is still on the door handle, but his eyes are looking right into mine. "A date?"

"Yep. I've got a date." He seems shocked, which I get. I'm a little surprised myself.

21

LUCKY

WHO THE FUCK IS SHE GOING OUT WITH?
   Is it someone I know?
   All I can do is cover my face with my hands and groan.
   If she's seeing someone, how long's it been going on?
   What if it's that twit from her building?
   I knew I should have kicked his ass when I had the chance….

BECKLYN

WHEN HE ASKED ME WHERE WE WERE GOING, I FIGURED HE WAS just making small talk since it was so quiet on the ride home from the gym. Usually, Deena would be jabbering on, but it was still way too early for her. Even after the workout, she found a way to fall asleep in the back seat using her gym bag as her pillow.

So, here I am at Brother's Bar & Grill with my date, Sam. And Lucky. Talk about awkward. I'd tell you it was a coincidence if there was any chance in hell that's what it was. I suspect Deena told him, since she's the only other person who knew. The truth is, I didn't think much of her question to Sam. Deena's nosey and a little protective of me. I assumed she asked him, "So, where are you taking my girl?" and "Are you doing anything else?" because she was making sure he wasn't taking me to some corn field somewhere. Except, now I know that's not the case. She was an informant rather than a friend.

I'm not surprised Lucky knows Sam—they both work out at Smiths. Sam is more into weightlifting than boxing or even kick-boxing, but I'm sure they've run across each other from time to time. When Lucky sidled up to our table, the two of them did that guy handshake and the back slap thing to each other like they were old friends. Sam, being a very polite person, invited Lucky to have a drink with us.

That was an hour ago. He even ordered food with us. They've spent the entire time talking about protein and supplements. It's annoying, and do you want to know what else it is? It's rude. Both of them are being very rude. And do you want to know something else? I'm not going to sit here another minute. The more I've thought about it, the angrier I've gotten.

Sam was my first real date. I didn't want to make a big deal about it, but it was significant, and my best friend, Deena, is part of this—this conspiracy.

I push my chair away from the table, and both men stop talking about creatine, whatever that is, and look up at me. Giving my best and fakest smile, I point toward the back of the restaurant. "Gonna use the ladies'."

"Oh, okay." Sam turns back to Lucky and keeps right on talking.

"Great," I mutter as I make my way in the direction of the bathrooms. Except, I don't need to go to the restroom. I look back at the guys and see they're still engrossed. I take the opportunity to do a little U-turn. I'm out the front door and walking to the bus stop before I know it.

Luckily, the bus arrives, and I hop on, swipe my metro pass, and am on my way home in no time. Sitting in the back, I frown, thinking of all the things wrong with tonight. Heck, my life, really. My anger has dissipated and turned into sadness. I wipe a tear from my cheek and will them to stop. I can't cry over any of this. It was just a date with a cute guy from the gym. There wasn't really a spark between us, but I thought he was nice.

It takes almost an hour for the bus to make the trek across town. When I step down at the stop nearest my apartment, I'm not surprised to see Lucky leaning on the hood of his car. As soon as I'm within earshot, he says, "That was a pretty shitty thing you did back there. Leaving your date at the restaurant like that."

I feel the flush of heat rising from my chest to my face. Oh, don't worry, it's not embarrassment. It's fury. I don't bother responding. Okay, yes, I have something to say. "Fuck you, Lucky."

My language must shock him, because his mouth opens, then closes several times as I pass him. Reaching for the handle on the front door, I feel his hand on my arm. And do you want to know something? For the first time in my life, I don't want Lucky to touch me. I need for him to step back. For him to go home and leave me the hell alone.

So, that's what I tell him. Those exact words.

Surprisingly, he does it. He pulls his hand away, and he steps back. I hear his footsteps as they retreat. Pulling the door open, I step inside. Now, I've got to deal with Deena. As far as I'm concerned, the three of them can go to hell.

It's been two weeks since my date. Well, I guess I wouldn't call it a date. In that time, I've barely spoken to my roommate, using short statements only when it's absolutely necessary. As for Lucky, he's been trying to drive me to work every morning, but I just walk past his car and head to the bus stop. He's sent me numerous texts apologizing for his role in the worst first date ever. (That's what I'm calling it.) Sam's been avoiding me altogether. I had a text from him that night asking me where I went. When I didn't respond, he didn't try again. Part of me thinks that's a good sign. Sam didn't seem especially into me. He was more interested in hearing what Lucky had to say that night, and part of me is just glad he's no longer a concern.

"You ever going to talk to me again, Foxy?"

I turn to see Lucky about five feet from me. I'm at the bus

stop outside Smith's Gym. My class is over, and I'm on my way home to shower and change for school. Hearing the nickname that I used to love only reinforces my feelings. While I'm tired of being angry with my friends, I'm not ready to forgive just yet.

"Probably not."

"You're going to have to talk to me at some point."

"Why is that?" I turn to face him.

"Your brother's coming to visit. He's staying at my place. You'll have to pretend—"

"I'm not going to pretend shit." I snap. "If he asks why I'm not talking to you, I'll tell him." Not like he'll care. Joe's really only interested in Joe. I know this because I've sent him numerous texts asking him how things are going out in San Francisco, but he's yet to respond to any of them. Correction, he replied to one with a word: Yo. That's it. I didn't even know he was coming home. Nobody tells me anything.

"Look, Becklyn—"

Just then, the bus pulls up, the doors creak open, and I step on. Perfect timing. Now I don't have to listen to any of his stupid excuses.

Except, when the bus pulls up to my complex, he's there. Like he is every morning. Throwing my gym bag over my shoulder, I start to walk past him without even looking. I guess he's had enough, because unlike other mornings where he just watches me pass, this time he's moving to the sidewalk to block my path.

"Becklyn. Stop." I don't. I step onto the grass and attempt to walk around him. "Becklyn. Please." Lucky's voice is soft now. He sounds sad, if that's possible.

Setting my heavy bag down, I turn to face him. This thing with him is exhausting. I just want to move on with my life. With my hands on my hips, I release a heavy sigh and ask, "What?"

"Look. I'm sorry, okay?"

I've heard that before. "Okay. Great. I accept your apology." He hasn't heard that yet.

"You do?"

"I do." Bending, I pick my bag back up and throw it over my shoulder. "Now, can we get on with our lives?"

Lucky's handsome face is all scrunched up in the middle like he can't understand something. "What does that mean?"

"It means I accept your apology." Duh.

"Are we back to where we were before?"

What the hell is he talking about? "Where were we before?"

"Friends." It wasn't a question, but there was a little bit of question in his voice.

"Sure." I shrug the best I can with my heavy bag on my shoulder. "We're friends."

Lucky sighs like he's relieved to hear those words. "So, you wanna come over for dinner?"

Is he crazy? "No. But, thank you." I've taken two steps when his hand wraps around my upper arm.

"Babe…"

My head slowly turns until we're looking into each other's eyes. "What?"

"Why won't you come to dinner? I thought you said things were back to normal."

"Did I say that? That things are 'back to normal'?" Yep, I sound like a total bitch. I'd love to tell you I can control it, but I can't. I'd also like to tell you I can just forgive and forget about all of this, but that's also a big ol' no.

"Yes."

"No." I shake my head. "You wanted to be friends again. We're friends again."

"We used to—"

I hold up my hand, and he stops talking. "That was before you ruined my very first date."

Lucky blinks at me.

"Yeah. That's right. My *first* date. For some inexplicable reason, you and Deena thought it'd be hilarious to screw it up.

You strolled into the bar, plopped down at my table, and took over, making it all about you." Saying this out loud is making me angry all over again.

"Becklyn, I—"

Waving him off, I finish by saying, "You broke some sort of code." I don't know what you'd call it, but he did. "A friendship code or something."

"Becklyn…"

I shake my head, because I'm done.

And I'm sad. I'm very, very sad.

23

LUCKY

How in the hell did I fuck this up so badly?

Oh, I know. It was when I decided to show up on what I now know was her first fucking date, turning it from something special into something more like a joke. Little did I know she would take it this way—as a betrayal. Because that's what this is to her. I know it. I did something that now seems irreparable. I've damaged us. And I have no idea how to fix it.

"What's up with Becks?" Joe asks me as he pulls a beer from my fridge. He's been here two days now and we've seen Becklyn once, by accident. I've sent her multiple texts letting her know her brother is in town, and the only response I've gotten is "Okay. Thanks."

"She's busy." While I'm sure she is busy, I don't honestly believe that's the reason she's blowing Joe off. It's because she doesn't want to see me.

Joe makes a scoffing sound. "Doing what?"

"Working. I told you she teaches the 5:00 AM KB class now."

"Yeah?" His response makes me wonder if he's been paying any attention to my messages.

"Yeah."

"Bet she's hilarious to watch."

What the fuck is his deal? "She's great, actually. They had to move her class to the large studio, it's so popular."

Flopping onto my sofa, Joe snickers. "Everyone loves to watch a train wreck."

"No." I shake my head. "She's really good." The only thing that's going to change his mind about this is to see it for himself. "We'll go in the morning. You'll see."

"Fuck that, man. I'm not getting up at the ass-crack of dawn to watch my sister crash and burn."

"Jesus," I mutter. "You don't know jack about your sister."

"And you do?" Joe's left brow is almost up to his hairline. His receding hairline.

"Yeah, man. I do."

He stares at me for several long seconds. All he's doing is blinking. And thinking. Anger flashes across his face, and I know what's coming. "You fuckin' my sister, Lucky?"

"No." I shake my head. "I'm not."

Joe slowly stands, placing the beer can on the coffee table. Without a coaster. "You got a thing for my sister."

That wasn't a question. I need to think about how I'm going to respond to it. I could lie and tell him that I don't have a thing for his sister, but I'm sick and tired of pretending. So, I go with the truth. I mean, if he decides to throw a punch, I'll let him land one. But only one. Running my fingers through my hair, I release a lungful of air. I'm doing it. I'm going to tell my best friend the thing I've been keeping to myself for years.

"Yeah, Joe. I like your sister." *More than like.*

Joe hasn't moved from his spot by the couch. He also hasn't spoken.

"Joe?"

Holding up his hand, he finally asks, "Does she know?"

That question makes me laugh. "Uh, no. She doesn't. Mainly because she's not speaking to me."

Joe's face morphs from pissed-off brother into a smirk. "What'd you do?"

What'd I do? What *did* I do?

"I, uh, fucked up."

"Obviously. Now I get why she hasn't bothered to see me."

Yeah, *that's* the reason. *That, and you're a dick to her most of the time.* But I keep that to myself.

"Tell me what happened." Joe sits back down and reaches for his beer. "Leave out anything that will make me want to knock you the fuck out."

So, I do. I tell him about her first date and my role in ruining it. He finds the whole thing hilarious, which doesn't surprise me. Joe's an asshole, to be honest.

After I finish telling him the whole story and her reaction since that night, Joe slaps his knee and says, "Well, you know what you need to do, right?"

Short answer? No. Long answer? No. "No."

"You need to *make* her forgive you."

"Make her forgive me?"

"It's what I'd do, because that girl can hold a fucking grudge."

That seems to be true.

"If her roommate was in on it, ten bucks says she's doing the same to her." He chuckles. "One time, I cut the hair on her favorite Barbie. She didn't speak to me for a fucking month. Not until I wrecked my bike, broke my arm. After that, she felt sorry for me and Barbie-gate was all but forgotten."

Something tells me he's wrong about that. If I asked her about her Barbie, my guess is she's still angry about it.

"So, you're saying I need to injure myself so she'll forgive me?"

"Well, I wasn't saying that. I was thinking more along the lines of a grand gesture, but yeah, maybe getting your bell rung would be enough." He snickers. "I'd be happy to knock you out in front of her." Joe shrugs. "If it'd help."

Snorting, I glare at him. "Like you could knock me out." Turning, I sit in the chair next to the sofa so I can think. "It's worth a try."

When I look up at him, his expression is serious. "You really care about her?"

"Yeah, man. I really care about her."

"How long?"

He wants to know how long I've had a thing for Becklyn? "Forever."

"Funny. Looking back, I can see it now."

"Yeah?"

"I should have punched your lights out a long time ago."

"Good luck with that." I snicker. "Your right hook sucks."

Silence hangs between us for several minutes, then Joe leans forward. Placing his beer on the table, he rests his elbows on his knees. "She's special. If you're only after—"

"No." I shake him off. "I can get that anywhere. I know she's special."

"Alright." He nods. "You have my blessing."

Why was that so easy? "Did you suspect?"

"The only thing I knew was that Becklyn has had a thing for you for years."

"She has?" I guess I can see why he'd think that. She used to look at me like, well, like I look at her now.

"Uh, yeah." Joe looks surprised. "That's why I know she'll forgive you." Pausing, he adds with a laugh, "Eventually."

Eventually? I don't know how much longer I can take this.

I'm a little surprised when Joe asks, "So, we going to Beck's class in the morning?"

"Absolutely."

"This is what we'll do." He smirks. "I'll 'accidentally' punch you. She'll get all concerned and come to your aid." He swipes his hands together like he's just finished something. "Bam. All fixed."

He used air quotes around that word "accidentally." There's nothing accidental about his idea. He's going to get that punch in if it's the last thing he does.

You know what? I'm going to let him.

"We'll be brothers," he says, walking into the kitchen to grab another beer.

"Excuse me?"

"I said…" He cracks open the can. "When you marry my sister, we'll be brothers."

Wow. Seven words I'd never thought I'd hear from Joe. Marry Becklyn?

I let those two words roll around in my head for a minute or two.

Marry Becklyn.

It sounds right. It feels right.

The question is, how does Becklyn feel? About me?

24

BECKLYN

Sure, I knew my brother was in town. I'd seen the text messages from both of them, but I knew if I made arrangements to see Joe, I'd have to see Lucky as well. It's not like I haven't seen Lucky. Of course I have. He's everywhere. Here at the gym, for example. He's continued to work out early in the morning, which makes it impossible to avoid him altogether. I've also seen him a bunch of times in our complex. He's taken to parking his car in front of my building, which is absurd because I know there are parking spots in front of five. Not only that, he also works on his car. A lot. Whenever I've walked past, the hood is up and Lucky's doing something to it. Plus, he's waxed it twice, as far as I could tell.

Deena says she saw him rotating his tires one weekend. I missed that.

And yes, I'm talking to Deena again. It was impossible to stay mad at her, thanks to her determination. She wore me down—exhausted me with all her begging and whining. She swore Lucky threatened her life if she didn't tell him where my date was, which of course I don't believe. On the contrary, I think the pair were in on it together. Deena was probably thrilled when Lucky approached her. She was convinced Lucky and I would come home from that whole thing a couple.

Ha. What a joke.

Not only are we not a couple, we're not even friends anymore.

And yes, I realize I'm the reason for that, but dammit, he made me mad. More than mad. I'm tired of him thinking he can just, well, just interfere in my life. And for what reason? As a joke? To make it so no guy will ask me out?

Okay. Don't say it. He's not the reason I never get asked out, but he did ruin the one time someone did, and that deserves my anger. Or wrath, as Joe calls it. Actually, my brother Chris calls it that too. And my mom. But, whatever.

So, now he's here. In my class. With Joe.

"Hey, sis." Joe says, throwing his arm over my shoulder. "Heard you kick ass at this teaching thing." He snickers. "Get it? Kick ass?"

"I get it." Turning to face him, I wrap my arms around him. "Missed you."

"Aw, that's so sweet." God, I hate sarcastic Joe. Almost as much as I detest bossy Joe. Also braggard Joe. And…

You get the idea.

With his arm still wrapped around my shoulders, he pulls me in closer. "You ever met my friend, Lucky?" Joe reaches out and grabs Lucky by the shirt sleeve and pulls him closer. "Lucky? Meet my baby sister, Becklyn." He squeezes me so tight I wince. "Becklyn, this is my best friend, Lucky."

"We've met," I grumble.

"Hey, Becklyn." Lucky sounds almost sheepish.

"Lucky." I don't know what else to say. Sure, I could tell him I'm not mad anymore, but that's not altogether true. I'm not *as* mad. How's that?

Doing my best to get out from my brother's tight hold, I say, "Well, look at the time." Making my escape, I press the button that turns on the sound system and place my headset on so the class can hear me. With confidence, I say loudly, "Let's go, people. Grab your gloves, find a bag. Let's warm up."

The class is going great. Better than great. After they moved me into the larger space, my class grew exponentially. To say I'm proud is an understatement. The fact that they've recently asked me to teach an afternoon class as well tells me I'm doing something right. Funny, it feels natural to teach, which makes me believe changing my major was the right thing to do. I only hope I like teaching high school science as much as I like teaching this.

Walking around the room, I check on some of my new students, making sure they're doing the exercises using the proper technique. No, I don't know everything about kickboxing, but I've continued to learn, thanks to the internet and with the help of the owner of the gym, Bryce Smith. He's a former MMA fighter, which means he knows his stuff. Once a week, he teaches an advanced class for his instructors and anyone else who wants to know more. That extra tutelage has given me more confidence as well.

"Alright, let's switch things up. Gloves off. Let's hit the floor." I like to mix up my classes with extra floor work doing things like push-ups, sit-ups, planks, that sort of thing. Sometimes, if I'm feeling especially vindictive, I'll call for burpees.

I hate burpees.

It doesn't happen often, but today seems like the perfect day for those. Joe deserves some torture, and Lucky definitely needs a little extra work. Not that he can't do burpees with his hands tied behind his back…. The guy is in tip-top shape for sure.

Today, I opt for a pyramid workout, which means we'll start with several exercises at five reps each, then build up and up and up until we're doing twenty reps each. So, I explain what we're doing and hear several groans and a couple expletives from someone in the back. It's okay. While I know people hate this, they'll be glad they did them.

Just to show the class I'm not completely evil, I get down on the floor with them. "Five each of push-ups, sit-ups or crunches if you'd prefer, skis, and finally burpees. At your own pace." More moans and groans from the peanut gallery, and I want to laugh but I don't. "Go!" I shout into the mic.

I'm not the greatest at all of these exercises either, but I'm getting better each day. I'm so much stronger than I used to be. "When you're done with the first five reps, jog in place." I do that so those people who are a little behind can catch up.

"Now let's do it again. Reps of six."

This time, I make my way around the room watching how everyone else is doing. I see Lucky from the corner of my eye right as he starts his burpees. God, he's perfect. And I'm not talking about his body. His form is amazing. He should be teaching this class. My brother? Not so much. I smirk when I see him struggling with the skis. He's sweating like crazy, which makes me smile. Wide.

Once everyone has made it through the pyramid, I give them a short break. "Grab some water, everyone." On my way up to the front of the room, my brother reaches out and touches my arm. Turning to him, I'm shocked to see he's still panting. His face is red as a beet, but he's smiling. "Jesus, Becks." He laughs. "You're a fucking tyrant."

"I am?" I feign innocence. "Why would you say that?"

"Just look at me."

I giggle at his words and at the sight of him. Movement to my right draws my attention. Lucky's standing nearby, watching us. And while Lucky has some sweat on his brow, he doesn't look like he's had a tough time. I can't seem to bring myself to speak to him, so I pat Joe on the shoulder and tell him to get his gloves on. Then, in my headset, I shout, "Back on the bags, people. Let's go."

2 5

LUCKY

SHE'S EVEN BETTER AT THIS CLASS NOW THAN SHE WAS A FEW WEEKS ago. Not only that, but her confidence is through the roof. It's sexy as fuck, let me tell you.

I just wish she'd talk to me. Her only word to me, so far, has been my name. One word. That's it. I'm getting desperate here. Maybe Joe's right. If I pretend an injury, maybe she'd throw me a goddamn bone.

Desperate.

That's how I feel.

The thing is, what's my injury? Joe can't very well punch me in a class like this. We're not sparring with each other. It's a high intensity kind of workout, but there's no contact.

"Damn it," I mutter to myself.

"What?" Joe says, moving closer to me. He's sweating profusely. I wish he'd stay on his side of the bag.

"How am I supposed to get injured here?"

"I've been thinking about that."

"And…" I'm getting irritated with him. He's supposed to be the big thinker in our friendship. So far, he's not proving his worth.

141

"What if I accidentally kick you in the nuts?"

"Accidentally?" And there's no fucking way I'd ever let someone kick me in the nuts, accidentally or otherwise. "You'd nut me?" I seriously can't believe he's suggesting that.

"What?" He seems sincerely shocked at my response. "You want the girl, yeah?"

"Yes." I hiss. "But I'd prefer my junk wasn't destroyed in the process." I mean, I have plans for my guys.

"Okay. Fine. Let me kick you in the back."

"My back?" I guess that makes more sense.

"Yeah. We're about to switch sides, so let me accidentally kick you in the back. You go down like a sack of potatoes, and she'll run over to see if you're okay."

Yes, I know this scheme is stupid. Ridiculous, actually. I mean, who'd believe I'd let that happen? I'm pretty good at this shit. With a sigh, I nod. "Okay. When we switch."

"Great." Joe smirks, and I'm not sure I like it.

When the music changes, so does our exercise. Becklyn, in her mic, tells us all to repeat the last exercises but switch to our left side. I'm about to get into position when pain shoots through my right side. "Fuck!" I shout. I drop to my knees as I reach back awkwardly, grasping at my ribs. "You fucker." I can't even look up at Joe, it hurts too damn bad. "You fucking broke my ribs."

"Lucky?" I glance up at Becklyn. Concern is written all over her face. "What's wrong?"

"Your stupid motherfucking brother kicked me in the ribs." I wince in pain. While I want to lie down flat on the mat, I fear I won't be able to get back up.

"I'm sorry, man. It was an accident," Joe says, sounding sincere… sort of.

"Let's go, everybody. Nothing to see here," Becklyn says into the mic. "Last round before we stretch. Get it done." Pulling off her headset, she kneels in front of me. "What hurts?"

I'm panting now. "Ribs."

I feel her hand touch my side gently. "Do you think they're broken?"

"Maybe." I also know if that's the case, the only thing they'll do for them is wrap them up tight.

"Can you get up?" she asks in a gently soothing voice.

My breathing is getting a little labored, which concerns me. Broken ribs easily puncture lungs, but I think it's more pain than anything else that's making me short of breath. "Yeah." With her hands on my left arm, I'm able to push up to standing.

"You gonna live, man?" Joe snickers.

I glare at Joe. That fucker. "When I'm better, I'm going to kick your ass."

"I'll be back in Cali by then. You'll have to fly out if you want that to happen. Bring it on, asshole." Then the jerk snickers.

He snickers. Doesn't he realize he actually hurt me?

He thinks I won't? "No problem."

Yeah, I'm going to kick his ass as soon as I can move again.

As gingerly as possible, I make my way to the outer edge of the classroom to a bench, Becklyn at my side. "Sit. Let me finish up here and we'll go from there."

"Okay."

"I've got it, Becks," Joe says, flopping down next to me, jostling the bench. I wince at the movement. "I'll take care of our boy."

"No. Get back on the bag. You're not done working out."

"Jesus," Joe gripes. "Tyrant."

"That's right, assface." She smiles at her brother. "Get back to work."

And for the first time in five minutes, I smile. "Yeah, assface. Get back to work."

"I'M REALLY SORRY, MAN."

That's about the tenth time Joe has apologized. "I know."

"And who knew it wouldn't work?" I hear him snort.

He's right. It didn't work. When class ended, she checked to see if Joe had everything under control. Of course, Joe said he did. I would've punched him if I could have. He did the damage so she'd take care of me, then he told her *he'd* take care of me.

Idiot.

"She must be really pissed at you," Joe says, opening up the passenger side door of my car.

Then there's that. "She is." So angry with me, she couldn't see past it to take it upon herself to nurse me back to health.

Fuck. Now all I'm thinking about is Becklyn nursing me back to health.

Nurses are sexy as fuck.

"Sorry I can't stick around to help you out, but I promised Mom I'd stay at home my last two days."

"I know." And honestly, I'm ready for him to go. He's a lot of work. "I'll be fine." Luckily, I only have one cracked rib. He's damn fortunate there weren't more, but I'm still pissed as hell at Joe.

"Maybe Becklyn will finally stop being a raging bitch and—"

"Hey," I say angrily. "She's not a bitch."

"She is if she can't get over that bullshit. I know that guy she went out with, and he's a tool. Too many roids, man."

He's not wrong about the roids, but I wouldn't call him a tool. I'd definitely call him not good enough for Becklyn, but nobody is good enough for Becklyn. Not even me.

Maybe especially not me.

No matter. She's mine, and I'm hers. She's just going to have to forgive me at some point, because those are the facts—no getting around that.

As soon as he's got me settled in at my apartment, he grabs his duffle bag. I watch Joe wave as he leaves my apartment. "Take care," he says with a smile.

"Sure." I do my best to smile back, but it's hard when I'm grumpy.

Nothing is working out the way I planned.

Not my life. And certainly not the most important part... Becklyn.

LUCKY

I WAKE TO POUNDING AND IT'S NOT MY HEAD. IT'S KNOCKING. From my vantage point, I see the door. I know it's about ten feet from where I'm currently lying on the couch. Ordinarily, I'd jump up and be there in a second, but not now. My body has been reclining on this same spot since I got home today, which means my muscles have tightened up, which also means my injury is going to hurt like a mother if I try to move. No, now I have to decide if the pain of moving is worth it. When the knocking starts again, I say, "Come in," hoping like hell Joe didn't lock the door.

My eyes are on the silver doorknob. If it turns, I know I'm going to be able to stay put. It does. Hurray.

"How's the invalid?" the sweetest voice in the world asks from just inside my apartment door.

"Becklyn?" Swear to god, it's a mirage.

"Yep. It's me." She's smiling at me. I can't believe it. Maybe Joe was right. If so, that makes him a fucking genius. Right now, the pain doesn't matter. What matters is that it worked. *She's here.*

I watch her move closer. She's holding a dish. "You hungry? I brought you some soup."

"Soup?"

"Don't get too excited. *I* made it, and I can't cook like you."

"I'm sure it's great. It smells good." No lie. It smells delicious.

"Chicken noodle. Mom's recipe."

I've had her mom's soup before. It's good.

"You hungry now, or do you want it later?"

My stomach growls loudly. "Now. Please."

Becklyn makes her way into my kitchen. Setting the dish on the counter, she opens and closes several cupboards. "Aha," she says, pulling down a bowl. Next, she finds a spoon and pours some of the soup into the bowl. "Gonna zap it in the microwave for a second."

"Okay."

All I'm doing right now is watching her. Staring, actually. I can't believe she's here. It feels like it's been an eternity since the two of us have seen each other, let alone been in the same room. Sure, I know it's only been a couple of weeks, but it seems much longer since we spent serious time together. The memories of last spring when she stayed over at our place and I made her dinner come to mind. That's the night she first boxed, and we watched a movie. A movie I'm pretty sure she hated but watched anyway. I've thought about that night many times. In many ways, it was the perfect date.

Hey. She thinks her first date was with what's-his-name. I think it was with me, that night. Think I can convince her of that?

Probably not.

At least not right now. Maybe I'll mention that down the road, after I've convinced her to give me a shot.

"Here you go." I watch as Becklyn sets a steaming bowl of soup on the coffee table in front of me. Next, she pulls a baggy filled with saltine crackers from her jacket.

It makes me chuckle. "What else you got in there? A glass of milk?"

"Ha ha. No." She glances back into my kitchen. "Speaking of…
what would you like to drink?"

"I've got water here." I point to my water bottle. "A spoon
would be good, though."

"Oh." She giggles. "Duh."

She jogs back into my kitchen as I pick up the bowl. Bringing
it to my nose, I take a whiff. "Mm, smells good, babe."

Babe.

I should probably hold off on calling her stuff like that, but it
just comes out automatically when I'm with her. It's like I can't
help it. *Stick with Foxy.* That's what I *should* do. For now, anyway.

Back in front of me, she holds out a spoon for me. "Hope you
like it."

With spoon in hand, I dip into the golden broth in search of a
noodle or two. When I've got what I need, I open my mouth and
taste. It's good. Not great. Not as good as Mrs. M's, for sure, but
no way I'm saying a damn word about that. "Mm. Really good." I
nod and smile up at her. "Sit." I use the spoon to point to the seat
beside me. "Want to watch something?"

"Oh." Becklyn starts to look nervous. "I'd better not stay."

"Why not?" Damn. I thought we were friends again. And
hopefully a whole lot more. I need to go for it. Nothing to lose,
right? "Please stay."

With a sigh, Becklyn takes a seat in the chair across from me.
I'm disappointed she wouldn't sit beside me, but baby steps. She
watches as I eat. To reassure her that I, in fact, love the soup, I
say, "Your mom would be proud of your attempt at her soup."

"Attempt?"

Oh, motherfucker. Did I say the wrong thing? "You know
what I mean. That you made her recipe. Honestly, don't tell her I
said this, but I think yours is better."

"You do?" Becklyn's face lights up.

Phew.

"I do. Yours has more noodles, for one, and that's the best part of chicken noodle soup as far as I'm concerned."

"Me too." She's scooted back into the chair now, getting more comfortable. Or at least I hope that's what she's doing.

"Take off your coat. Stay a while." Sure, that's a cliché, but I mean it.

"I can only stay for a few minutes. I've got a paper to write." She rolls her eyes.

"Oh? What's the topic?"

Unzipping her coat, she pulls it open and slides if off her shoulders, saying, "English 207. It's a creative writing assignment that's supposed to be something fictional and in first person. I'm really not sure what to write." Placing the bowl up to my mouth, I pour the last drops of soup in. Becklyn must be pleased, because she's smiling when I set the bowl on the table. "There's more if you want some?"

"I'm good for now, but I'll definitely eat more later."

She smiles with pride. "Good."

"So, your story…." I lean back in my seat. "What if you wrote a love story." Those words just slipped out of my mouth involuntarily, but now that they're out, I'm thinking this is genius.

Her face shows no expression whatsoever. I keep going. "About a girl, a beautiful girl who's funny, sweet, smart, and a pain in the ass."

She arches her brow. She's getting a hint about where I'm going. "Sounds fictional already," the smartass states.

Holding up my hand, I scowl to get her to stop talking. I'm not sure why I think that'll work. It rarely does with Becklyn. "The guy in the story is sort of good-looking but not too bright."

That got a smile out of her.

"He doesn't see what's right in front of his face." I look into Becklyn's eyes. "Not for a long time."

The girl hasn't moved or said a word. Good.

"Until one day, he finds this girl at home on the night of the big, fancy ball."

"A fancy ball? When does this story take place? Regency times?" Her tone is sarcastic. I'm not sure I like it.

Ignoring it, I shrug. "Sure. That sounds fun."

"I'm no Jane Austen."

I'm not sure who that is, but I might as well pretend. "Who is, really?"

"Jane Austen," Becklyn deadpans.

"True." *Note to self, look up Jane Austen.* "Anyhoo…"

"Anyhoo?" She snickers. "Are you okay? Are you taking pain medicine or something?"

"Nah, I hate that shit." I give her a friendly glare. "And stop interrupting me. I'm on a roll." I pause then repeat, "Any*hoo*…" This story is awesome. Well, as long as it has a happy ending. "This handsome but clueless man stops over to this woman's house to discover she's all alone, wearing her pajamas, eating her weight in popcorn."

Becklyn crosses her arms and leans back in her seat. "Sounds like the girl knows how to enjoy a quiet night at home." I'm about to continue, but she adds, "And did they have popcorn in Regency England?"

Valid question, but I've got the answer. "They found popcorn in the pyramids." At least, I seem to recall they found it there. Or maybe that was oats…. I frown at her. "Stop changing the subject."

"Fine." Her sigh is sort of adorable. Especially when it's accompanied by a pretty pout.

I look at her, then down at my hands. She's making me lose my train of thought. "Where was I?"

"Popcorn. Pajamas."

"Right. When he sees her reading from a ye olde book while in her pajamas eating popcorn…"

Becklyn giggles but doesn't interrupt.

"…he knows right then and there that not only is she special but she's also his."

I spoke too soon. Becklyn's not going to let that one go. "All it took was her eating popcorn and wearing her pj's? Sounds a bit far-fetched to me. In my experience—"

My turn to stop her. I give her some side-eye while I'm at it. "In your experience?"

"Yes. In my experience, guys don't just *realize* they've been clueless."

She's right. I didn't realize I realized it then until much later. "What about this… instead of her relaxing at home, she's crying."

"Nope." She shakes her head. "I won't write about a sobbing heroine."

Wow. She's really making this difficult. "Hm, let me see…" I raise my arm to run my hand through my hair and wince. Every move I make hurts.

"Give up?" She smirks.

If she's asking if I give up on her, on this, then no. "I've got another idea."

"Good. Because this class is giving me fits."

"Our girl is strong and self-assured. Also, she doesn't realize how beautiful she is."

Becklyn snorts while scoffing. "Yeah. Right."

I'm not even going to respond to that. "She's beautiful, and she doesn't know it. Deal with it," I say in a rather perturbed tone. "She also doesn't realize she's in love with the handsome but clueless man."

"Mm-hm." She's crossed her arms again. "And what, pray tell, does this gorgeously clueless man do to help her see?"

"Well, obviously he kisses her." To add some humor, I finish that sentence with, "Duh."

I watch the blush creep up from Becklyn's neck to her cheeks. She's not about to let that stop her from contradicting me, though. "Oh, right. One stupid kiss is supposed to convince her that he's got a thing for her?" She adds a lovely eye roll to the end of that statement, and I don't like it. Not one bit.

"Sometimes a kiss is the key to the whole story."

"And sometimes it isn't." She scoots to the edge of her chair, then pushes herself up to standing. "I've really got to go."

Damn it. I thought this was working. I guess not. Mimicking her move, I scoot to the edge of the sofa, but I'm unable to push myself up. I try, but it hurts too damn much. "Here," she says, stepping over to me. "Let me help you up."

Taking my good arm, she helps support me as I use my legs to stand. When I'm on my feet, I look down at her. "Becklyn?" My voice is pretty much a whisper.

"Yeah?"

Bending down, I get as close as I can without actually doing something she won't understand. I place my hand on her neck. My fingers are touching those sexy curls, and my thumb is resting below her chin. "Sometimes a kiss is the answer."

Without missing a beat, she asks, "What was the question?"

I swear she's holding her breath as I say, "Babe. Take my car keys." Hell, I'm not sure why I'm avoiding her question. Maybe it's because she's not ready to hear what I've got to say. To be safe, I'm just going to shelve the whole subject.

"Take your car keys?"

"I can't drive. Not for several weeks. So, take the keys."

"No." She shakes her head. "I can't."

"Yes, you can. I'm not using it. I don't like you catching the bus that early in the morning. Plus, if I need something, you can run out and get it for me." I give her my best smile. "You'd be doing me a favor."

Becklyn stares at me for a bit. "Fine." Her sigh is one I've heard so many times, it's sort of endearing now.

"Great."

Walking her to the door. I'm still tempted to kiss her but decide to hold off. The next time I kiss my girl, it's going to be the one that seals the deal.

2 7

———

BECKLYN

The second I step into my apartment, my phone chimes.

Lucky: Hey, will you pick me up some milk tomorrow?

The urge to growl is strong. Why do I get the feeling that taking his car keys is going to be the worst thing I've ever done?

Lucky: 2% please. There's some cash in the glove box. Use that.

He leaves money in his car? That's not smart.

Me: You shouldn't leave money in your car. Someone could break in and take it.
Lucky: I'm Lucky Ganetti. Everyone knows my car. Who'd fuck with it?

True. Like I said, people think he's got ties to the underworld. He doesn't.

Me: Anything else, your highness?
Lucky: Not right now, but if I think of anything, I'll let you know.
Lucky: Wait. Yes. Bread. Whole wheat. I'll send you a link to the kind I like.
Lucky: And a tomato. For my bread.
Lucky: Cheese. Sliced.
Lucky: American
Lucky: No. Swiss
Lucky: …

I stare at my screen as those little dots move, knowing he's typing something else. Yep. I'm going to regret taking his keys.

SLIDING OUT OF LUCKY'S MUSTANG THE NEXT MORNING, I SMILE. "I could get used to this." I got a whole fifteen minutes of extra sleep this morning just because I knew I had wheels. It's too bad I've got a list of groceries about a mile long to pick up for Lucky after my classes today. So much so, I have to stop at Lucky's apartment to get more money.

No worries. I don't mind. It helps me procrastinate, because, admittedly, I've got things I *should* be doing, like writing that stupid story. But helping Lucky out is much more enjoyable, especially since I get to see him again.

Now before you think too harshly of me about forgiving and forgetting about the date stuff, I think I may have taken my silent treatment a little too far, but it couldn't be helped. Once it started, I couldn't shut it off. Does that make sense? It took something like Lucky getting his ribs cracked to give me the opportunity to set things right. Well, at least get things a little back to normal. Deena and I made up a while ago, and that's mostly because Deena is relentless. Lucky didn't try very hard.

Or did he?

And does it matter now?

I'm going with no—it doesn't matter now. The reality is my feelings for Lucky haven't changed one iota since I was a teen. Just being around the man makes me weak-kneed. Even being mad at him has done nothing to quell those feelings. It took him being hurt for me to realize how much I still care for the idiot. Helping him out now is easy. Trying to keep my feelings to myself, well, that's not.

And then there's last night… I could have sworn he was going to kiss me, but that's ridiculous. The last time he kissed me, he ran away so fast and for so long, it made my head spin. No, I need to remember—we're friends. That's it. Nothing more.

Accepting that is harder than you'd think. I mean, I've literally been dreaming of a life with Lucky Ganetti for three years. Even to the point I've named our three children. Sure, that's typical teen girl stuff, but the sad part is I just came up with the names last summer. A summer Lucky spent in Chicago doing his internship. His *entire* summer. Mom and Dad kept asking about him. Whenever Joe called to check in, they'd inquire about Lucky's whereabouts. All Joe ever said was, "He's working in Chi-town."

I assumed he was going to stay there. When Deena told me she saw him in the management office of our apartment complex, I had to wonder why he was back. He graduated with Joe. Heck, I half expected him to move to San Francisco. Joe wanted him to, I know that for sure.

He didn't, though, and I haven't asked him why that is. And why did he come back to school? Sure, having a master's degree is probably wise with his major, but he seemed set to get to work.

Oh, hell. What do I know?

Maybe I should just ask him about it?

Yeah, Becklyn.... "I'll ask him."

2 8

LUCKY

"Here you go. Last of your groceries, Your Highness."

I feel terrible. Becklyn's made two trips down to my car and back with my grocery order. I should have thought this through. Did I really need a ten-pound bag of potatoes? No. How 'bout the gallons of milk and orange juice? No.

Well, okay. Yes. I needed those two things, but I could have done without the potatoes.

"I'm getting a second workout today," she says with a laugh.

"Sorry, babe." I watch as she sets the final few bags on my kitchen counter. Then I watch as she starts to put things away.

"Where do you keep your cereal?" She stares at the box of Lucky Charms. My absolute favorite, and my cheat food when I'm working to build muscle.

"In the cupboard next to the fridge." Close to the milk.

Once everything is put away, Becklyn reaches for her jacket. "Can you stick around for a little while?"

"Oh." She looks down at her coat, then up at me. "A few minutes, sure."

Good. Now, all I need to do is make good use of this time. I need to tell her—she needs to know how I feel about her.

159

"Let's sit." I point to my living room area.

I move to the chair in the hopes she'll take the couch. I've got a plan, you see.

"You must be pretty bored." She snickers. "To want my company."

That's not funny.

"I missed you." Yeah. I said it.

"Sure." Becklyn's smirking, but I know her better than she thinks.

"I did. I missed you. I have plans to cook dinner for you if I can get you to hang out for a bit."

She doesn't respond to that. Instead, she asks me a peculiar question. "So, why did you decide to come back to school? I figured you'd move to California or stay in Chicago. You had a job offer, right?"

Joe must've told them all that.

This is it. This is my chance to tell her the real reason I came back.

"Becklyn…" I look down at my hands. My fingers are intertwined, and I'm leaning forward a little, my elbows on my knees. It's one of the few positions that don't hurt. "I came back for you."

There. I said it.

"Excuse me?" Her voice sounds squeaky. Her face is hot pink.

I look directly at her. Our eyes meet. "I mean it. I came back for you."

Becklyn's shaking her head. "You expect me to believe that. Af-After last spring?"

"No. I don't expect you to believe it, but it's true. After I kissed you that night, I had some real soul-searching to do."

Her scoff-slash-snort is a bit off-putting but understandable.

Reaching my left hand out, I touch hers. The one that's on her right knee. "Just hear me out. Yeah?"

"I'll try. But I smell bull crap."

"No. I'm not making this up. Just let me tell you my story."

"Your story?"

"Yeah. *My* story."

So, I do. I tell her that the man in my fairy tale from yesterday was me. And the fancy ball was her prom. And that it took me two years to realize that was the moment Becklyn stopped being that annoying little kid and turned into a beautiful, smart pain in the ass.

I don't think she appreciated that last part.

"I'm not a pain in the you-know-what."

"I like that part of you."

"Uh-huh. Sure."

"The thing is, Becklyn, I have feelings for you. It's why I ruined your date. The thought of you out with another guy, well, I wanted to punch that guy out."

That must've gotten her attention, finally, because her face softens as she asks, "You did?"

"I was so fucking jealous."

"You were?"

"Hell yes, woman. Shit, the thought of you with someone else… it-it makes me crazy."

"I haven't been out with anyone else."

"Thank fuck for that."

"So, what are you saying?"

"Come 'ere." I use my hand to wave her to me. She stands up slowly and steps closer. Reaching out, I take her right hand and give it a little tug. She ends up standing between my open legs. I want to reach out with my right hand, but honestly, even lifting the thing hurts. So, I use my left hand and run it up her arm to her elbow as my eyes move up from her thighs up over her stomach and almost past her breasts. They stop there for just a second, then move on up to her beautiful face. "Baby girl. What I'm saying is—" I suck in a deep breath, because these words are important. "—you're mine."

Her gasp catches me off guard, but in a good way. "I'm yours?"

"And I'm yours. If you'll have me."

"You're mine? If I'll have you?"

I tug her elbow until that sweet little ass of hers is on my knee. When she's there, I reach up and move a curl out of her eye. "Exactly. You're mine and I'm yours. If you feel the same."

"Since prom?" Her voice is shaky. I hope that doesn't mean she's going to cry. I'm not sure I can handle a crying Becklyn.

"Since prom."

"Wh-Why didn't you tell me?" Her eyes are turning shiny, and my fear is realized the second a sparkling drop slides down her cheek.

I reach up and wipe it away, but another one follows. "Don't cry, sweetheart." *Please. I hate it.*

"You didn't speak to me for four months."

She's referring to the end of spring semester and this summer. "I had to figure things out." I had to talk to Joe. And that didn't happen until earlier this week. Now that it's out there, I'm starting to worry about something. She hasn't actually told me how she feels. Does she feel the same? I know Joe thinks she's had a thing for me for years, but I'm not so sure. Especially now that she's doing her damn best to stand up—to pull away from me.

I let her go.

When she's up, she starts pacing back and forth in front of me. "So, you stayed in Chicago all summer long just because you had feelings for me?"

"Yes."

She does her scoff with a side of snort. "You expect me to believe that you had such immense feelings for me, you stayed away."

I push myself up to my feet. "I had some thinking to do." I had to figure out my way around Joe. "And the work kept me in the city."

She stops moving and turns to face me. "So, what did it? What finally made you see that you-you wanted to come back here?"

She's not saying the obvious. That the reason I'm back is because of her. "It was the first week at the job in Chicago. I knew I had to come back, so I called one of my professors to ask about graduate research. A week later, I was accepted into the program with a research assistantship. Two weeks after that, I found this apartment."

Becklyn is staring at me. Her hands are on her hips, and her chest moves up and down as she breathes deeply. The silence is concerning. I've known her long enough to see that she's not happy. So, I do the only thing I can think of: I step close enough so I can wrap my left arm around her, pulling her in close. Our eyes meet. "Give me a shot, Foxy." She blinks. "Please?"

Releasing air, she says, "I swear to all that's holy, Lucky Ganetti, if you pull another runner like you did last spring, I'll break more than one stupid rib."

"Noted." I chuckle and then smile so big, it hurts. Sliding my hand into her hair, I place my thumb beneath her chin to lift it enough for our lips to meet.

That's when I kiss her. I kiss her like she's the last person I'll ever kiss again.

Because. She is.

When I pull back from the kiss, Becklyn's eyes meet mine. They look as though they're searching for something. Perhaps she's looking for truth or sincerity or I don't know what. Leaning in, our lips touch again, and for the first time in my life, I feel like everything is going to be okay. That's a feeling I haven't felt since, well, since I was five. When my mom was still around. She had a way of making everything right. Becklyn does the same thing for me.

I kiss her softly, her top lip, then her full bottom lip. Moving right, I kiss the corner of her mouth and do the same on the left. Moving up, I kiss her left cheek, then her right. I'm not sure why I'm doing it; maybe it's because I feel like worshiping her. She's the most important person in my life. Something I hadn't real-ized until she stopped talking to me.

Actually, no, I take that back. I realized it last April. After I kissed her outside her dorm and then walked away for months. I knew then that part of me was missing.

Her.

But I thought it was for the best. That she deserved better than me. But when I discovered she was living in the same apart-ment complex as me, I decided to believe fate was involved.

"Fate's a thing, right?"

"Huh?" she asks, sounding a little dazed.

I hadn't realized I'd said that out loud, but that's okay. "Fate. It's a thing, right?"

"I guess." Becklyn shrugs.

"Yeah. It's a thing."

"Do you want to know what else is a thing?" She grimaces, then titters.

"What?"

"You stink."

"I do?" I raise my left arm and smell. Now it's time for my own grimace. "I haven't showered?"

"Today?"

I shake my head.

"Since yesterday?" Her voice is squeaky. She attempts to pull away from me, but I'm not ready for that just yet. Becklyn's nose crinkles up into an adorable expression of disgust.

"Sorry." I chuckle, then regret it. "I wasn't about to ask your brother to help me in the shower, since I can't really get undressed." I point to my right side. "Can't get the shirt off."

"Oh." She's thinking.

I'm watching.

"I, uh, can help you get undressed." She glances at my face quickly, then her eyes return to my right arm. "If-If you want."

"That'd be great." I grin. "You sure?" I'm not even hesitating.

Sure, I'm asking if she's sure, but I'm not about to let her walk away. I need a shower. My hair is sticking up all over the place, and I smell. Something I hadn't really noticed until now.

What?

I sweat a lot. I'm used to it.

"Sure." Becklyn's face flushes, which makes me smile. She's pretty in pink.

"Come on." I take her by the hand and pull her toward my bathroom. Once inside, I stand in front of the sink vanity facing her. I raise my arms slowly and wait for her to help me off with my tee.

"Tell me if this hurts." Becklyn's voice is soft and sincere.

"I will." Gazing down, I watch as her little fingers grasp the bottom edge of my shirt and slowly push it upward. I'm holding my breath in an attempt to keep my dick from reading too much into this.

In my head I'm telling him to stay down. That this isn't one of those times he can stand at attention.

Think about something else. My head is working overtime to come up with something. *Think about... England?*

No. I shake my head.

"What's wrong?" she asks. Her hands stop moving for a moment.

"Nothing. Just thinking about England."

With a giggle she repeats, "England?" Her hands continue.

"Yep."

"I'd love to go to England someday. And Paris."

"I'll take you."

Her hands stop again. "You will?"

"I will." *Honeymoon.*

What the ever-loving... *honeymoon?*

"Well, I'll hold you to it."

"Good."

When the shirt gets up over my pecs, Becklyn asks me to bend down. Bending hurts, so I opt to squat. Doing that enables her to get it up over my arms and off. Lowering my arms, I glance down at my workout pants, then up at her. Arching my brow, I'm giving her a signal she's going to have to help me with the rest. "I can't really bend."

"Oh."

Hot pink. That's the color of her cheeks right now. "Sorry." Am I sorry? Yes. I am, because I don't want her to feel uncomfortable. "If you want, you can close your eyes."

"I've seen a penis before, Lucky."

"You haven't seen mine."

"Well, they're all the same." She looks away from me, adding shyly, "Right?"

"If you say so." God, I want to laugh, but like I said, she looks seriously embarrassed.

"Come on, braggy. Let's get this over with."

Now, I laugh. "Not exactly the words a guy likes to hear…."

That makes her snicker, which eases the tension in the room considerably.

"Turn on the water for me?"

"Sure." Reaching into the bath/shower combo, she turns on the faucets, then uses her fingers to make sure it's the right temperature before she flips the switch for the showerhead. When that's done, she turns back to me, looks down at my pants, and sighs. "Here goes nothin'."

It's my turn to laugh.

When she touches the tie that holds my sweats up, I feel a flash of electricity run downward. Goose bumps pebble my arms and legs as she tugs on the string.

"Seriously, Becklyn. If you just want to get them down over my thighs, I can get the rest."

"No." She shakes her head. "This is nothing."

She cracks me up. "Trust me. It's *not* nothing."

Muttering, "Shut up, Lucky," she tries to loosen my pants, and holy fuck, I think this might be the sexiest thing I've ever seen, because the damn tie is knotted, which is frustrating the fuck out of Becklyn. Her little growls are making my dick hard, which is going to shock the shit out of her when she finally gets my pants down.

It can't be helped, honestly. That's the effect she has on me.

"Got it," she says, sounding relieved.

Once it's undone, I feel her fingers slide just below the elastic. As she pushes downward, the trail her fingers are taking on my body make my skin feel alive. Hot. I shouldn't look down. I shouldn't want to watch, but I can't help it. I need to see. When she's got my pants down over my hips, she hesitates for a split second. Then, quickly, they're past my rock-hard cock down to my upper thighs.

"Wow" is all she says.

"Sorry." Not sorry.

"Why?" Her eyes are on my dick, which only makes him harder.

"Why am I hard?" I want to laugh or chuckle, but I know I shouldn't. "Because you make me this way."

"I do?" Her focus is still on little Lucky. (Well, he's not little. Wink-wink.)

"You do." Reaching down, I place my thumbs on either side of my boxer briefs. It's enough to make her realize she's been staring for a bit. "Not a lot of hot water. I need to get in."

"Right." She nods. "I'll, uh…"

"Help me with my boxers?"

"Seriously?" she whines. "Come on, Lucky."

"You're going to see him eventually. You may as well, as you said, get it over with."

"No." She shakes her head. "You did not just say that."

"I did." I smile. "And I'm going to see *you*." Fuck. I can't wait for that day.

"God," she mutters. "Fine."

"Turn around, babe. Sincerely, if you feel uncomfortable…"

"I'm fine. Honestly." I hear her mumble after that, and I'd swear she said something about "finally seeing what all the hoopla was about." Something along those lines, anyway.

Her fingers find their way inside the waistband of my underwear. This time, it's me holding my breath. She works quickly. My shorts are pushed down to the floor, enabling me to kick them off. "Now, help me wash my hair?"

"Are you for real?" She's turned away from me now, giving me her back.

My voice becomes kind of whiney when I admit, "I can barely raise my arm, babe."

"Fine." Mumbling, she adds, "I'm going to kill Joe."

"Get in line, sweetheart. Get in line."

I guess she thinks that's funny, too, because she cracks up. Which makes me laugh right along with her. Once her laughter slows, I carefully step over the side of the tub into the shower. I moan at the feel of the water as it sluices down over my body; it feels so damn good.

"Get your hair wet, then bend down a little."

I do as she asks, except I can't bend very far. When her fingers find their way into my hair and she starts to work up the suds, I moan again. Sure, I love when someone plays with my hair, but nothing compares to how it feels when it's Becklyn touching me.

"You need to quit making those noises." Her voice is husky. Like she's turned on.

Rinsing out the soap, I look down at her. Her eyes aren't meeting mine. They're looking at my dick.

"Becklyn?"

"Huh?" Her head jerks up. "What?"

"Is this okay? I *really* don't want you to feel uncomfortable." That's the last thing I want.

"I'm not uncomfortable." She mumbles something I can't quite make out. "I've got brothers."

"What'd you say?" She didn't just say that. "I'm not your fucking brother."

Her voice cracks. "Believe me. *I know*." She reaches for my body soap. "Come on. Let me wash your back."

I'm not going to turn down that offer.

When her palms touch my skin, I move back so I'm as close as I can get. I'd like nothing more for her to wash my entire body. Then I'd like to return the favor. I close my eyes as she works the soap over my upper back, then down my spine to my lower back, working the liquid soap into my hips. I feel her fingers touch either side of my abs. When her palms move over my glutes, my ass, I flinch.

"Sorry," she says, pulling her hands away. Reaching back, I take hold of her hands and place them back on my butt.

"It feels good. Your hands on me, Becklyn. It feels perfect. Don't stop."

"Oh."

She moves the soap around my ass a little longer. "You've got a great butt."

"Thanks."

"You've got a great *everything*."

"So do you."

"Ha," she says sarcastically, and it pisses me off.

Turning to face her, I reach for her chin, lifting it until we're making eye contact. "I mean it."

"Mine is nothing like yours."

"Well, thank goodness for that. Your curves…. I've dreamed about them."

She glances down at herself. The white tee she has on is soaked through. "Oh, crap." Becklyn attempts to tug it away from her body, but I reach out and stop her. "Let me look."

"Lucky…"

"Pretty bra." It appears to be a pale pink color. Lacy. As I stare, her nipples peak. Her chest is rising and lowering like she's having trouble catching her breath. Reaching for my towel that hangs next to the shower, I wrap it around my waist and ask, "Becklyn?"

"Yes."

"I've got this." What I've got is a hard-on that won't quit. Not until she leaves. "Grab a towel. I've got some T-shirts in my top dresser drawer if you want to put on something dry."

"Right." She looks at the wall, then at the ceiling, doing her best to keep her eyes off me.

"Baby." I reach out and touch her face. "Look at me."

She glances down at my terry-cloth-covered dick again. "At my eyes, honey. Look me in the eye."

That gets her snickering again. "Oops." But she does it.

"I never want you to feel uneasy around me. I know this was a bit fast, the shower and all…"

"No. It's fine."

"For the record," I smirk, "I can't wait until we're there."

"There?"

"Yeah. When we get to the place where I get to help *you* in the shower."

"Lucky…." She blushes.

"I mean it. We're just not there yet."

"No." She shakes her head, and her curls bounce from side to side. Her hair is so damn sexy. "We're not there yet."

"Soon, though."

"Soon?"

"When you're ready." I want to be sure.

"Okay."

"Now, grab something dry out of my drawer." Because the sight of her wet T-shirt is more than I can take. Have mercy.

2 9

———

BECKLYN

SURREAL. THAT'S THE ONLY WORD THAT COMES TO MIND AS I search his top dresser drawer for a T-shirt. I opt for one I remember him wearing all the time back home. I guess you'd call it a classic band tee, black with the logo from the group U2. I know he loves them. I remember him listening to them a lot.

As I'm about to lift my wet shirt off, I turn and watch Lucky step into his bedroom. "Oh, sorry." He must see what I'm doing.

I have a decision to make here. I can either skitter away, maybe go into the bathroom and change, or I can just do it now. In front of him.

With bravery I didn't know I had, I turn slowly, facing him. My hands are still on the bottom edge of my white shirt. His eyes haven't left me. They're now gazing down at the bottom of my shirt. I swear he's holding his breath.

"Becklyn." His voice comes out sort of gruff. "If you do that, I'm going to…"

"What?" Since when did I get so daring? "What are you going to do?"

He doesn't hesitate. "I'm going to want to touch you at the very least."

171

Perhaps I should give this more thought. Am I ready for Lucky to touch me?

Long answer? Yes.

"Lucky Ganetti," I say as I slowly raise the shirt over my stomach that's still pretty soft. "I've been waiting for you to touch me since I was old enough to know what that meant."

"Babe…" Lucky's chest is moving up and down, fast.

My shirt is right below my breasts. Below my best and prettiest bra.

Yeah, I thought about it. I changed into it before I went to the store.

Without another thought, I drag it over my chest, past my neck, and off. Tossing it to the side, I let my arms lower to my sides. The two of us stare at one another for way too long. As far as I'm concerned, the next move is his.

He doesn't disappoint. His stride is long and determined. If there wasn't carpeting in his room, I suspect I'd hear his feet pounding. He's in front of me in no time. "You're fortunate."

Oh, wow. He's not one of those guys, is he? Sure, I joked about him being braggy, but it was a joke. "Fortunate?"

"If my rib wasn't cracked, this would end up with you in my bed."

Well, shoot. I forgot about his stupid rib. "Why is that fortunate?"

"We're not there yet."

"You may not be—"

"We're not there yet."

He's so sure… "So where *are* we?"

He looks down at my chest. I watch as his left hand moves up to my waist. I feel its warmth as it moves up over my ribs to right below my right breast. "Can I touch you, Becklyn?" His voice… *gah*… is soft and husky. Sexy. Unbelievably sexy. There's a little shakiness to it as well that makes this moment so much better than anything I ever imagined. It's like he's turned on and nervous.

Just like me.

3 0

LUCKY

"Yes. Touch me, Lucky."

Reaching out, I let my fingers skim over her bra. Once. Twice.

"Lucky." Becklyn's voice is husky.

"Feel good?"

"Yessss."

I move my hand to the other side and repeat the touch. With two fingers, I pinch her, not hard. The move makes Becklyn squeak, so I stop. "Did that hurt?"

Her head shakes back and for. "No. Do it again."

"Fuck." My side hurts, but I don't give two fucks. I get to her fast. My mouth is on hers in a searing kiss. I'm so fucking turned on, I'm about to lose my shit right here, like a fourteen-year-old boy.

I swear, I've never been this turned on.

My tongue is in her mouth, sweeping and searching—for what, I'm not sure. All I know is she tastes sweet. Not like candy but like a rich dessert. I move my mouth to the side of her neck and whisper in her ear, "I need to touch you, Becklyn."

"Yes. Do it."

I've got her pretty pink bra pushed down beneath her breasts

175

a second later. I take a moment to look. To stare. "Fuck." Her tits are what dreams are made of—full and round and *Jesus...* Bending, I take one into my mouth and suckle. "So fucking sweet," I say as I move to her other one. She's arching into me, her fingers running through my wet hair.

"I fucking need you, Becklyn."

"Yes." Her leg wraps around my left side, and her center presses up against my painfully hard dick.

She's... she's everything I've ever imagined, only better. But this can't go much further. Not this time. I can make her feel good, though. Kissing her neck, I slide my hand down from her breast to her stomach. "Your skin is so soft." It comes out as a whisper, partly because I'm reveling in the feel of her. The feel of her is... amazing. It's more than just her skin. I don't ever remember anyone else making me feel so charged, like there's electricity running between us. As my fingertips push just beneath the edge of her jeans, I pause and look into her eyes.

She nods slightly.

I use three fingers and undo the button. Next, I grab the zipper tab and slowly drag it down. The room is silent except for the erotic sound of the zipper.

I place my palm on her lower abdomen and slide it down. Down beneath the elastic of her panties to her center. "Wet," I mumble as I take her mouth again. Jesus, the word "plunder" comes to mind. I want to be deep inside her. All of her. Her mouth, her cunt. Knowing she's untouched—okay, assuming she's untouched—is driving me insane. "Am I the only one who's touched you like this, Becklyn?" *Please say yes. Please...*

"Yes."

"Fuck." I groan in her ear as I suckle her lobe into my mouth. "So wet." Using my middle finger, I circle her clit once, twice, three times. Her body is moving with me. She's pressing closer. "You want me, baby?"

"Yes. I want you, Lucky."

"Gonna make you come now. Okay?" I know she's close. She's moving faster, and her breathing has gotten out of control. Pressing a finger inside, I'm careful to be gentle, moving it in, then out. My thumb swirls around her clit, placing pressure there on each pass.

"Lucky. God," she says, throwing her head back. I take the opportunity to latch onto her neck. Probably leaving a mark. "Yes," she cries. "Don't stop."

"Never."

Pumping into her three more times, I feel her tighten around my finger. She's squeezing me so much, all I can think about is what that's going to feel like when it's my cock inside of her. Imagining that makes me dizzy.

No. I need to focus on her. On her pulsing around my finger. On her face. It's flushed. On her mouth, her lips open, and on her eyes. They're dilated and hooded.

Fuck. It's sexy.

"Wow." She finally speaks. "That was an orgasm." Her head lowers until she's looking at me. "Right?"

I'm a little shocked. I figured… "You've never made yourself come?" I assumed every girl…. Well, that's a dumb thing to assume. This is Becklyn we're talking about. She was probably waiting for…

It suddenly hits me. "Becklyn?"

"Huh?"

"Are you waiting…?"

"Waiting?"

"For your wedding night?"

She's staring at me. No words have been spoken by her. Not yet anyway. Still none when she slowly closes her legs in front of me.

I get the feeling I've said the wrong thing. "Becklyn?"

She pushes herself away from me. I reach for her, but she pushes my hands away. When she walks around me in search of her shirt, I follow her. "Babe?"

Turning, I watch her slide on my U2 tee. After it's over her head and pulled down over her gorgeous upper body, I've got to say, it's never looked better.

"No. I'm not waiting on my wedding night."

Okay. That's a relief. I guess. "Good."

"Good?"

"Well…" Shit. I need to consider my words here. "Yeah. Good." Because the truth is, I don't want to wait. I've waited long enough. However, if she needs to wait, then, I will. So, that's what I say next.

It must be the right thing to say because she smiles. "I never intended to wait. It's just never happened." Her face suddenly changes. Fear. She looks scared. "Does it bother you that I've never…?"

"No." I'm quick to respond. "Absolutely not. I mean… to be honest, I'm glad I'll be your first." And her last.

"You sure?"

The good part of that statement is she's given this thought and she's chosen me. She's chosen me.

"Hell yes, I'm positive." I wrap my one good arm around her and pull her into me. "I'm honored." I clear my throat, because I'm getting a little emotional. "I'm sincerely honored, Becklyn."

"Well, don't get all sappy on me." She snickers. "I'll probably suck at it."

"Impossible. Not after what we just did. You coming is the best fucking thing I've ever seen."

"Oh." The blush is back. With a vengeance.

BECKLYN

"Where the heck have you been?" Deena's got her hands on her hips and her foot tapping. "I thought you were just taking some groceries over to Lucky's place." She glances at the clock. "That was three hours ago."

Crap. I should never have told her about Lucky. About his injury, his car keys, and about his groceries. She's never going to let this go. She's been saying all along that I should just forgive the guy. That he was in love with me and jealous over my date; I just couldn't believe her. Not this time. And while it made sense, her reason for him showing up at my date, I'd been there and done that with him before.

But, now… things are different.

So much different.

And she is my best friend and biggest cheerleader. (Besides my mom, that is.) I owe it to her to give her some information.

"I had to help him shower."

Okay, that was kind of, sort of evil. It's going to get her all excited.

"You what?" She practically screams it.

"I helped him shower."

"Wait one gosh-dang minute…" She's got both hands wrapped around her ponytail and her foot's-a-tapping. "You saw him naked?" Now she's jumping up and down. "You saw freaking Lucky Ganetti naked. Didn't you?" She's stopped moving. Frozen in time. Waiting on my answer.

I can't leave her hanging…

Well, I can… for a minute or two.

"That all depends."

"On what?" she hisses. "Spill, bitch. Spill right this damn minute."

"Oh, all right." I move into the living room and sit on our loveseat. Crossing my legs, I place my palms on my knees.

"Fucking speak," she shouts. "I swear to God, Becks, I'm going to—"

"Yes!" I shout. "I saw him naked."

"And?" she plops down on the floor in front of me. "How big is he?"

"Compared to what?" That's a serious question. She knows I'm a virgin. I confessed one night over a bottle of cheap wine.

Holding up one finger, she jumps up, runs to the kitchen, and is back in seconds. "Let's compare." She clicks around on the phone and then holds it out to me. I see a screen full of penises. About twenty of them. All shapes and sizes. My mouth is suddenly dry.

"You want me to tell you which one looks like Lucky's?"

"Yes."

"I can't." I hold her phone out to her.

"Why the hell not? I told you about all of my—"

Hookups. That's what she means. She hasn't told me about her boyfriend's, although he's a dick so I really don't want to know about his, well, dick.

"You're not going to tell me?"

"I can't." I nod at the phone. "Because Lucky's was…" Oh, God. I can't say it.

"His was what?" Deena's practically on top of me now. "What?" she screeches.

"His was hard. Pointing up." I use my finger to demonstrate.

Deena's voice changes. It almost sounds reverent. "He had a hard-on?"

"Um. Yes?"

"Hold on." She types away at her phone, then hands it to me again. I know what's coming, and I'm afraid. Very afraid. "Here."

Knowing I'm not going to get beyond this until she knows, I grasp her phone and look at the images of at least twenty erect penises. "Wow. So much variety." Then I snicker, because, well, I'm nervous and embarrassed and an idiot. Finally, I spot one that seems accurate, but it feels wrong to tell her--like I'm giving up one of Lucky's secrets or something. Looking over my shoulder, I shrug. "I'm not seeing anything."

"Oh, you're so full of it." She grabs the phone and points at one. I look down at the penis in question and shrug. "Maybe."

"No. Fucking. Way." Deena's voice has gotten loud. "You have got to be fucking kidding me."

My 'maybe' didn't work the way I'd hoped. I glance at the phallus again. "I'm not sure. It's possible." I look at Deena.

Then, she does something strange. She flops onto her back on the floor and proceeds to laugh. She laughs her butt off.

When she's finally calmed down (about five minutes later), she rolls onto her side and slaps my leg. "Only you'd end up with a guy who's gonna split you in two the first time you do it."

"Huh?" I grab the phone again and stare at the dick. "You think?"

"Oh, yeah." Deena pushes herself up off the floor. Reaching for the phone, she slides it into her back pocket. "Remind me. The next time I go to the store, I need to pick up a first aid kit."

And that's all it takes for me to do what Deena just did. I laugh my butt off.

"WHERE'RE YOU HEADED?"

"Going to Lucky's."

"I hope you finally do it. Jesus. It's been two weeks since the whole dick pic thing and you're *still* a virgin."

"He's got a broken rib."

"How long does it take for those to heal, for crying out loud?"

"Weeks. The internet says weeks."

"Perhaps you should put some pressure on that rib and see what happens."

"No." I want to laugh, but I can't. "I'm not going to hurt him."

"Look." Deena gets close. Too close. Placing her hands on my face, she looks me dead on. "If you don't get that man naked again, I'm going to die."

She cracks me up. "Deena," I say through giggles, "you aren't going to die if I don't have sex with Lucky tonight."

"I suppose you're going to do what you've done every single night since you saw his frank and beans..." Deena's eye rolls are legendary. This one is no exception. "You're going to eat something, then watch Netflix. Only you don't actually 'Netflix and Chill.'" She uses air quotes. "You actually watch Netflix."

"And?" I say, a little exasperated. "He's got a broken rib, Deena." Also, I haven't mentioned to her that most nights we end up making out like horny teens and that his hands have been all over me and mine have been on him. Heck. Take last night, for example. I used my hand to make him... God, I'm blushing at the memory. I used my hand to make him come, and it was stinking hot. I sort of can't wait to try it again. "It'll happen when it happens."

"Just hurry, will you. I'm dying over here."

"Why don't you go see what's-his-name." She knows I don't like her boyfriend. He's seriously a jerk.

"His name is Marcus, and you know it."

"I try to forget." It comes out as a mumble, but I know she can hear.

"Well, if you must know, I cut him loose."

Thank goodness. But I need to be a friend. "You did? When?"

"Last week."

"And you're just now telling me?" What if she's been hurting all week…? "You okay?"

"Yeah. He was cheating on me."

"*No.*" Seriously. "He was? How'd you find out?"

"Caught him in the act."

"What an idiot."

"Right?" She chuckles. "Funny thing was, I stopped over to visit. His roommate opened the door and told me Marcus was in his room. I walked inside and down the hall. I didn't even bother knocking." She lifts her shoulders. "Why would I?"

"You wouldn't."

"Right. Anyway, he was lying there getting his knob polished by some skank in a red bra and purple undies." Deena visibly shivers. "They didn't even match."

I'd like to laugh at that, but she's completely serious. Worse than her boyfriend getting a blow job? The woman wasn't wearing matching lingerie. "Then what happened?" Because I know something else happened.

"He saw me; he looked shocked. Then he started in with the 'this isn't what it looks like' shit."

"*No.*" I sound shocked because that's the dumbest thing I've ever heard. Who says something like that at a time like that?

"Yes. He did." She sighs. "So, I just held up my hand to stop him and said, 'I've been trying to figure out a way to let you down easy, but you did it for me. *Byeeeee.*' And then, I turned and walked out, leaving his door wide open."

"Wow." She's seriously my hero.

She's not finished though. "Funny thing happened on the way out, though."

"Did he chase you down naked?"

"No." She taps her chin. "His roommate was waiting by the front door."

"He knew what you were walking into?"

"Probably. But that's not the weird part. He handed me his digits and said, 'Call me when you're ready.'"

"What'd you say?"

"I asked him, 'Ready for what?'"

I repeat. She's my hero. "What'd he say?"

"He said, in a very deep voice, 'For *me*.'"

"Oh. My. God." I practically squeak. I'm starting to sound like her. "That was hot."

"Right? And let me tell you. His roommate is *not* ugly. I'd go so far as to say he's almost as hot as Lucky." She winks. "Almost."

"What are you going to do? Are you going to call him?"

"Not sure." Deena starts playing with her hair. "It's odd though. I think I talked to Blaze more than I did Marcus. We'd hang out while I waited for the dipshit to get home. He's cool. Funny. And like I said, smokin' hot."

"Blaze?"

"Nickname. His last name is something like Blazek."

"As in Theo Blazek, the quarterback of the U of I football team?"

She shrugs. "No idea." And oddly enough, I believe her. "After my round with the hockey guy, jocks haven't been on my radar. Too self-absorbed."

"You should call him."

"I'm not ready for another relationship. I'm going to the party at the clubhouse this weekend to find a hookup. That's all I need for now. You're going with me, right?"

"Oh. Well...." I'd forgotten about that.

"Bring Lucky along."

"I'll ask him about it tonight."

"Cool." She sounds chipper. "Awesome."

3 2

LUCKY

I can't believe she talked me into coming to this stupid party. I'd seen the signs up all over the complex about it, but I'd ignored it. It's not like I don't enjoy a good party; it's just I don't enjoy one being thrown by a bunch of undergrads.

Now, before you think I'm a snob, that's not it. I'm older than most of these yahoos, and it's obvious that I'm over this kind of thing. But Becklyn isn't. She's just getting started, so I'm going to do what I can to support her. Not to mention the fact that there's no way I'd let her go to one of these things without me. Not now. Not anymore.

Not after the last couple of weeks.

A couple of weeks of us spending every evening together like an old married couple. Shit. I'm smiling just thinking about it. The only thing that's different is that we haven't slept together. Literally or figuratively. I've walked her to her place every night. At her door, I've pressed her up against it and kissed her like I'm never going to see her again. It feels that way sometimes; like she's my world and the minute she walks through her door, everything stops.

Sure, that sounds overly dramatic, but I'm just telling you my take.

"You made it." I look up and see my girl racing toward me. She nearly knocks me down as she throws herself at me, her arms wrapping around my neck. I wince a little, but there's not a lot of pain. Plus, I've got it wrapped up pretty tight. I was worried one or more of the yahoos I mentioned would bump into me.

"Of course I made it."

"Isn't this party crazy?"

I look around the place and do a mental calculation of the size of the group. "Pretty crazy."

"Deena's around here somewhere." She's up on her tiptoes, doing her best to see over the crowd. I spotted her roommate a little while ago.

"She's hanging with Theo Blazek."

"She is?" Becklyn starts to jump up and down in an attempt to see the quarterback. "She didn't tell me she called him."

I shrug, because I have no idea what she's talking about. And honestly, I don't really care. I'm only here for her.

"Where are they? She said he was almost as good-looking as you." She winks at me. "Almost."

"Good to know." I raise my arm and point to the far corner of the room. "Over there."

"Let's go. You want to meet him?"

"Uh." How do I tell her that I already know him? I guess I'll just say it. "We're friends."

She stops suddenly and turns to face me. "You are? With the starting quarterback of our football team?"

"He's not that good." Okay, he's pretty good. He may even go pro, but we're going to need some offensive linemen who can stop the blitz.

"I thought he was really good." Becklyn looks confused. "So, if you know him, is he a good guy?"

"He's cool." And he is. We work out together from time to time at the university gym. I've had a beer or two with him as well. "I don't know how he is with his dates, though." We don't get personal.

"'Sokay." Becklyn sounds a little tipsy.

"You been drinkin' babe?"

"I had one," she holds up one finger, "beer."

"You gonna have more?"

She shakes her head. "No. It's warm and gross. I switched to water."

"Good to know."

I take her hand and lead the way to the back corner, where we find Deena and Blaze. The name everyone calls him but he hates. He's used to it, though. As soon as he sees me, he raises his hand, and we do that guy shake. You know the one where we slap each other's backs?

"'Sup Lucky?"

"Just partyin' with my girl, Theo." I step back and wrap my arm around Becklyn. "My girlfriend, Becklyn."

She looks starstruck, and I'm not going to lie, I hate it. But I get it. "Nice to meet you, Blaze."

"Call me Theo, yeah?"

"Sure." She gives him her sweetest smile. "Sorry."

"No worries. Blaze gets old."

"You didn't tell me that," Deena interrupts.

"Sorry, babe. I don't mind it."

"No." She smiles at him. "Theo is nice."

The pair gaze at one another like they're alone. They're not. Case in point, several dudes approach and want to get pictures with the star, essentially ending our little chat.

"Later, man," I say, taking Becklyn off to our own little corner. On the way, we stop by the keg, where we each grab a bottle of water. Just as we're about to find a secluded spot of our own, I feel Becklyn's hand slide out of mine. When I turn, she's being wrapped up by that guy. The one that lives next door to her. I'm immediately on alert.

"Becks. Wow," he says with his arms around her. When he steps back, he's staring down at her shirt. "You look hot as fuck, girl."

"Oh." Her cheeks get a little pink. "Thanks."

I take a moment and check her out. She's got on a pair of tight jeans, ones that on a normal day, I'd love. Tonight, at this thing, not so much. On top she's got on a long-sleeved V-neck tee with our school logo. It's snug on her but in all the right ways. It's also kind of low-cut. Nothing too scandalous. I've seen other women wear the same thing, but Becklyn makes it better. It could be because she's got more up top, or it could just be that she's got the curves needed to make an ordinary tee look fucking fantastic.

I watch in horror as the douchebag reaches out, takes Becklyn's hand, and tugs on it. "Come over here. Let me introduce you to my bros."

His bros? What the fuck?

"Oh, well..." Becklyn sounds conflicted. "I'm here with my friend Lucky."

Her friend?

Her fucking friend?

I'm immediately incensed. I just introduced her as my *girlfriend* to Theo "Blaze" Blazek, and she's calling me her friend? What the ever-loving fuck?

"Babe." I decide to end this right now. "Time to go."

"What?" She looks up at me. "Go? We just got here?"

"Yeah, and I'm done with this." This bullshit.

"Dude. If you don't want to be here, then go. Becks and I will—"

"Do not. Finish that sentence."

"Lucky? What's going on?"

I glare at her. And what does she do? She stares back, but there's confusion on her face. Doesn't she see what she did?

Doesn't she realize what this tool's doing? So, I do the only thing I can do so things don't escalate. "My ribs hurt. I need to go."

Her face morphs into concern. "Oh, no. Did someone run into you?"

"Yeah." Nobody ran into me, but I'm about to punch someone in their fucking smug face. That's going to hurt my ribs.

"Let's go, then."

"Becks." The twerp is practically whining. "I've been waiting to party with you for weeks."

"Well." She looks up at me. "I could walk him home and come back."

Okay. Now. I'm pissed.

Beyond pissed.

Does she not get it? Doesn't she see what she's doing? She's supposed to be with me.

I guess not. I can take a hint. "Fuck this." I turn on my heel and head straight for the door. "How could I have been so wrong about her?"

"Lucky?" I hear her voice from somewhere behind me. I don't bother stopping. Why would I? "Lucky!" Her voice is louder now. When she grabs hold of my arm, I'm tempted to rip it free, but when I look down at her, all I see is worry on her pretty face. "What's wrong?"

"What's wrong?" I growl. It can't be helped. "What's *wrong*?"

"Yeah. What's wrong? Why are you so mad?"

We've drawn attention to ourselves. I can't have that. I won't make a scene at this stupid party. Don't get me wrong, I don't give two shits what these assholes think of me, but I won't have them talking about Becklyn.

Taking hold of her hand, I pull her with me out the door and across the lawn to building five. Pulling the key card out of my pocket, I slide it through the reader and hold the door open for her. I follow her up a set of steps to my floor, unlock my door, and hold it open for her too. Once inside, I drop my keys on the table, turn, and I'm on her before she can even speak. I've got my arms around her and palms on her ass. Lifting her, I press her up against the wall next to the door. "You and me are gonna have a long talk after."

She looks terrified. "After?"

"Yeah. After."

"After what?"

Instead of talking, I lean in and kiss her lips softly. "After I show what I meant when I said you're mine." I pause. "And I'm yours."

"Oh. I see."

"Do you? Because the shit you just said back there says otherwise."

"What do you mean?"

I guess we're having the talk first. It makes sense to do it this way. I set her down on the ground and take her hand again, leading her through my living room to my bedroom. We haven't slept together, as I said, but we've spent a good amount of time on my bed. We've had some good talks there too.

Once I'm in my room, I pull off my tee and strip out of my jeans, leaving me in only my boxer briefs. "Your turn." I nod to Becklyn.

Like it's old hat, she strips off her shirt, then those tight jeans. I smile when I see her black bra and matching panties. "Pretty," I say, reaching out so I can touch the pretty lace trim on the bra.

"It's new."

"I like it."

"Me too." She smirks. "It makes me feel confident."

"As it should." I let my hand glide down over her shoulder and down her arm. I feel her skin prickle beneath my fingers. "So soft."

I watch her walk over to the bed and sit. "So, as you were saying…"

I have to think for a minute. What was I saying?

"Why were you angry at the party?"

Oh. Now I remember. With hands on my hips, I say with meaning, "You told that idiot I was your 'friend,'" I say with finger quote things.

"You are my friend."

"No," I snarl. "I'm your boyfriend. Big difference."

"Ah. I see." She smiles at me. "You were jealous again."

"The fuck? Of course I was jealous again. I'm your man. You're my woman. You don't call me your 'friend' in social situations. Especially when some motherfucking guy is hitting on you."

"He wasn't hitting on me. He's—"

"He. Was. Hitting. On you, Becklyn. Jesus." I run my hand through my hair. I swear to you, she's going to be the death of me. "I know you're a little naïve sometimes, but you had every single fucking guy in that place staring at you. I thought I was going to have to throw down with half the place."

"Don't be ridiculous."

"Sweetheart." I sigh. She cannot be serious. "You have no idea how fucking hot you are, do you?"

"Hot?"

"Yeah, babe. You're a stone-cold fox. You're hot as sin. You're fucking Marilyn."

"Marilyn? Who's she?"

"Monroe, babe. Marilyn Monroe, only you're better."

"She was blonde."

"So. Nobody cares what color her hair was, honey."

"Well. Sure. I guess."

We're both quiet for several moments. I've been doing my best to calm down using breathing exercises I use while boxing. It's helping. "Becklyn, my love..."

"My love?" She smiles.

"My love. Yes. You're my love. With that being said, whenever we're out together, it'd be great if you acted like you were *with* me. I mean, if I have to beat up a room full of men, so be it, but it'd be best if you pretended to be with me."

Becklyn's voice has grown soft. "I am with you. I've always wanted to be with you."

"You have?"

"Yes." She rolls her eyes. "You know I have."

"No. I didn't know that." Not for sure.

"I just figured you didn't want a clingy girlfriend."

"Ordinarily, no. But we're not talking about any ordinary girl-friend. I want everyone to know you're mine. I want to hold your hand and have my arm around you so guys like your neighbor know you're taken."

"I see."

"Don't you want the same? Don't you want other women to know I'm with someone? That I'm with you?"

"Yes." It looks like a lightbulb went off. "Of course. I can't deal with the Tiffs of the world."

Me neither. "Then we understand one another?"

"We do. We're a couple. When we go places, we behave as such."

She makes it sound like she's reading relationship directions from a how-to book. It works. "Yes. We're a couple. You're mine, and I'm yours. Which means you don't walk me home and go back to a party to hang out with another guy."

There's shock on her face. "Right." She nods. "I can see how that must've looked to you."

"Think of it this way. How would you feel if I'd said that to a girl?"

"I've have kicked you in the nuts, then gone for her with my talons out."

"See?"

"I see. I guess this is all new to me."

I find myself standing in front of her. "I get it. We'll have to take each incident as it occurs. We'll talk it out."

"Incident?" She laughs. "You mean when I screw up?"

"Exactly. We'll call them teachable moments."

She looks up at me, and then her eyes travel down. Down over my chest, past my abdomen to my boxers. "Is this a teachable moment?"

"I believe it is."

"Okay, Lucky… teach me something."

Jesus. She's going to be the death of me.

At that moment, one I'll remember for the rest of my life, she rolls onto her back and reaches her arms out to me. "Come on, Professor. Show me what you've got."

Oh, I'll show you…

33

BECKLYN

WHAT AM I DOING? WHO AM I? I'M CERTAINLY NOT THE SELF-conscious girl I thought I was. I mean, I just stripped out of my clothes and walked over to the bed like I owned the place. Now I've positioned myself in as sexy a pose as I could think of and said something provocative. I called him "professor," for crying out loud.

I'm not sure if I can give kickboxing all the credit, but it's helped. My body is the same as it used to be, only slightly firmer. Honestly, I think it's him. I've no doubt he thinks my body is beautiful. I saw it in his eyes, in his reaction that first time. There was almost a reverence. I see it again now as he places a knee on the bed. "Wait," I say as Lucky crawls on the bed. "Your ribs?"

"It's been three weeks...."

"Don't they hurt, though?"

"No." He leans down and kisses my mouth.

"If they hurt, we shouldn't—"

"I'm fine, beautiful."

I blink at him, thinking about his words. "You sure?"

"Well, right now, my dick is the only thing that hurts. If we stop, I'll have double the pain."

"Oh."

"Yeah." He kisses me again. "*Oh.*"

I glance down at his, well, his penis. He's taken off his boxers. *When did he do that?*

It does look rather painful. And angry, if I'm being honest. And big, but you read that in every romance book, right? Well, trust me, he's quite large. Let's see, how do I describe it so you get a better picture. How's this… have you ever seen a baseball bat?

I giggle to myself. He's certainly not as big as a baseball bat. I close my eyes in an attempt to think of something equivalent to Lucky's erect penis.

"What's up, Becklyn?"

"Huh?" When I open my eyes, he's staring down at me.

"Why are you squeezing your eyes shut like you want this to be over?"

"No." I shake my head. "I was trying to think of a way to describe, your, um…" I point down to his hardness.

He pushes back onto his knees so we're both staring down at it. "It's not as big as a bat," I say out loud and regret it the second Lucky starts to laugh. "Shut up."

"A bat, huh?"

Frowning, I repeat, "I said it *wasn't* as big as a bat. God. You're so arrogant."

"You said it, not me." He glances down at himself. "I'd say a Maglite heavy duty flashlight."

I give him my best stink eye, because "You came up with that awfully quick. Have you given that some thought in the past?" I look around his room. "You have one of those Maglite things, don't you?"

"Maybe?"

"Let me see it."

Reaching into his nightstand drawer, he pulls it all the way out, reaches into the back, and grasps the item in question. I take it in hand and hold it out close to his penis. "Actually," I lean in closer. "Not that you need to hear this, you braggart, but I think you're bigger than this."

"Yeah?" He smirks.

"Stop it." I examine him again. "You're a little thicker but not quite as long so take that as you wish." I roll to my side and set the flashlight back into the drawer.

I marvel over the fact that we're both naked and laughing as we compare his dick to a flashlight.

"I don't remember ever having this kind of fun in bed. And hell, we haven't even done the deed yet," Lucky says, smiling over at me.

"You're right. This is fun. In the last few weeks, we've had fun messing around." But now this is getting serious because his hand moves down my neck, over my collarbone to my left breast. He skims his fingers over the tip, and I moan.

What'd I tell you? Serious.

His hands on any part of me brings my body to life, but my breasts are extra special. I look up and marvel at his focus. He's touching me while watching my face. I want to keep looking at him, but the sensations force me to close my eyes so I can concentrate. When he pinches my nipple, my moans grow louder. I love it when he does that. Leaning down, he takes my nipple into his mouth and licks and sucks until I'm rolling to get closer to him. "Lucky, don't tease."

"Teasing makes it better."

"It does?"

"Definitely. I need to make you dripping wet. Teasing does that."

"Can I tease you?"

"Not if you expect me to last, Foxy."

Since I'm not sure exactly what he means by that, I decide to pretend I know what I'm doing. (I don't, by the way.) Leaning over, I press my lips to his.

"Kiss me again, Becklyn."

Gah! Lucky's voice is so damn sexy. It's deep and husky and just… just hot. Not to mention, it's a little bossy. Ordinarily, I'd probably ignore his orders, but not today. Not right now. "Like this?" I scoot closer, my breasts brushing his chest. There's a smattering of hair on him that tickles a little. Mostly it adds to the overall sensual experience. When my lips touch his, Lucky's hand slides across my neck. His fingers weave through my hair, holding me in place. He takes over the kiss, and I let him because my focus is on all the other sensations and urges I'm experiencing. Like the fact I want to touch him. Everywhere.

Placing my palm on his pectoral, I sweep my fingers over his nipple and feel it harden beneath my fingers. I let my hand wander down over his abdominals to the line of dark hair that starts at his navel and ends, well, at his Maglite.

While I'm doing that, his mouth and tongue are doing magical things to my mouth, neck, and now my breasts. He's good at all of this. With practice, I think I could be good too.

"You gonna touch me, Foxy?" he asks, skimming his own hands over my body.

Deciding not to answer with words, I wrap my hand around him and marvel at the feel of it. He's hard, but the skin around his shaft is soft. It makes no sense.

"Like this." Lucky wraps his hand around mine and proceeds to show me how to touch him. Our hands move up and down together. "Yeah, honey." Lucky's starting to pant, and I like it.

Placing pressure around him, I pump up and down once more. "You like that?" I know he does.

"Fuck. Yes."

Getting a rhythm, I'm fixated on watching his face and body react while also paying close attention to his penis. Liquid is seeping out of the tip. I know people lick that. I've read about it. I'm not ready to do that, though. He doesn't give me a chance, anyway, because before I know it, I'm pushed onto my back and he's above me. "Can't wait. You sure about this, love?"

"I'm sure." Am I, though? Really?

Our eyes meet, and I see two things in his. Confidence and love. Yes. I see love in his eyes. "I'm sure."

Lucky reaches over and dips his hand into the nightstand drawer again, retrieving a condom. We talked about birth control and being tested one other time. "I'm on the pill," I remind him. I'd explained that it was for my cycle. He wasn't surprised. He said he'd heard that before. I was surprised he was so easy to talk to about it. Having grown up with Joe, I know how to word anything about my period so he wouldn't get all weirded out. "Cycle" is one word Joe can handle.

"I've never gone without before." Lucky's giving this some thought.

"It's okay if you're not comfortable…."

"I am, though. With you, I'm comfortable." We gaze at one another.

Lucky tosses the condom somewhere to my right. The next few minutes are filled with sensations I'll never forget. He uses his hands, his mouth, and his body to bring me to the brink of another orgasm. When his finger circles my clitoris, I feel the telltale signs of my release, but he stops before I get there. Instead, he places his, well, his Maglite at my entrance. "I'm afraid this may hurt, Becklyn."

"I know. It's okay. I'm ready, Lucky."

"I'll go slow. Yeah?"

"Yeah."

I try to keep my eyes open, but when I close them, the feeling of him entering me is heightened. He's big, and he's filling me. Opening my eyes, I look down at us. "How much more needs to fit in there?"

I realize how ridiculous my question is and start to laugh. It can't be helped.

Lucky's expression starts off as fierce but quickly turns into the opposite. "Shit, Foxy." He chuckles. "To answer your question, all of 'it' *will* fit in there."

"Whoa." I glance down at us again. "There's no way…"

Lucky loses it then. He throws his head back and laughs so loud and so deep it starts me going again. "What?" I ask between gales of laughter. Tears are dripping down my cheeks then down onto the pillow behind me.

"Woman," he says, shaking his head. "You're going to be the death of me."

"Sorry."

One second later, Lucky presses in a little more, which stops my laughter because stuff is getting real.

"You okay, honey?"

"Yeah." I want to tell him to just go for it, but I'm scared.

He's wincing as he says, "Not much further."

I smirk at his words, but when he presses deeper, pain shoots through my pelvis. "Oh, wow. Ouch."

"Sorry. Sorry." He's stopped moving. Leaning closer, he kisses me gently. "I'm sorry."

"N-no. It's okay." It's already dissipating. "It feels okay."

"You sure?"

Wiggling my hips, a little, I nod. "Yes. Better."

"Thank fuck." That's when Lucky pulls out and presses back in. He repeats this move over and over and over again until I'm writhing beneath him.

"Yes. Lucky."

"Jesus. You feel amazing, Becklyn."

I love all of his terms of endearment, but there's something about hearing my actual name in this moment that means something special. "I love you, Lucky."

"I love you more, Becklyn."

And with that, we do something that they only write about in books. (At least that's what Deena says.) We both come at the exact same time.

34

BECKLYN

"O-M-G. You did it. Didn't you?"

Looking up from my textbook, I see a very disheveled Deena in the kitchen drinking old coffee from the pot I made earlier this morning. It's now noon. "Did what?"

She slams the cup down onto the counter. I frown because a) I know she's figured it out, and b) I'll have to clean up the coffee that just sloshed out of the cup onto said counter. "You did I-T, *it*. The deed. The horizontal Mamba… unless he did you up against the wall, then it'd be the vertical Mamba." She starts playing with her hair and tapping her foot.

Never good.

She's not done. "Coitus, sexual congress, sexual rela—"

Holding up my hand with the hopes she'll stop, I resign myself to telling her. "Yes, Deena. I did it. We did it."

Rushing from the kitchen over to the sofa, she plops down next to me, reaches for my book, and unceremoniously drops it onto the ground. "Spill. I want to hear this from beginning to end. Don't leave out one thing."

"Deena." Sure, my voice is whiney. Because I don't want to tell her everything.

"No." Her head moves from side to side. "Don't you dare try to get out of this. I've waited two years for you to pop your cherry—"

"Eww." My face is scrunched up. It's my "I'm disgusted" look.

"Oh, stop." She slaps my knee. "You know what I mean."

I do know what she means. It doesn't mean I like it. "I'm not going to tell you everything, because, well, because it was special, and I want to keep it that way."

Deena's face suddenly morphs from something rabid, like she's going to attack me if I don't talk, to something much softer. She tilts her head to the left and says, "Awwwww. He was gentle?"

I wouldn't necessarily say that, but when we did it the first time, definitely. The second time, not so much, which is okay because I asked him for more. I smirk at the recollection. Lucky absolutely knows what he's doing in bed.

Deena clears her throat, reminding me I've gotten lost in thought. In the memories. "Let me just say this." I pause and turn to face her fully. "He was perfect."

She stares at me for a good minute. "That's it? That's all you're going to tell me? He was *perfect*?" Standing up from the sofa, she grabs hold of her ponytail and starts to slide her hands down the length. Pacing in front of me, she says, "I need more than that. This isn't how it works. You don't just say something like that and then not expand on it. I mean..." She stops in front of me. "I'm dying to tell you about my night with Theo, but I'm not going to do it until you reciprocate."

She's got a point. I'd love to hear about Theo. The fact that he didn't come out of her bedroom with her just now intrigues me. "Did he sleep over?"

Crossing her arms, she glares down at me. "Not until you spill the beans on you and Lucky."

Patting the seat next to me, I hope she takes the cue, because this feels like that time I got caught looking at one of Joe's naughty magazines. Both of my parents stood over me as I cowered on the sofa for that lecture.

Fortunately, she does sit. I've decided to approach this differently. "He told me he loved me."

"Oh. My. God." She squeaks, then claps, then bounces up and down all while seated. "What did you say? You told him you loved him too, right? Because I know you love him. I just knew he loved you. God." She's barely taken a breath.

"I told him, yes."

Deena's eyes start to get shiny like she's going to cry. Deena never cries. Ever. "Then…" She sniffles. "It really was perfect."

I reach out and hug my best friend. In her ear I repeat what she just said. "It really was perfect."

"Good," she whispers back. "That's what I wanted for you. I wanted it to be perfect."

And now it's my turn to sniffle.

"And hot. I wanted it to be fucking hot. Tell me it was hot."

I giggle in her ear, because now she's got me wrapped up tight. "It was so hot, girl. Swear to you. When I get more comfortable with all of it, I'll tell you more. But, for now, I'm just still processing everything."

Pulling away, she nods and swipes away a couple of tears on her cheek. "Fair enough." Standing, she heads back into the kitchen, picking up her coffee cup like none of that happened. "When you're ready to talk, I'll tell you about Theo."

"Not fair," I grumble. Because I really do enjoy her bedtime stories. (And by that, I mean tales of her escapades in bed.)

"Let me just say this." She sets her cup down, places her palms on the counter, and leans in. "I didn't have sex with Theo Blazek."

"What?" Good thing I wasn't eating or drinking anything right then, because it would have ended up all over the coffee table.

Her smile is huge, from ear to ear. "He turned me down."

Oh, no. Wait… "And you're happy about it?"

Shrugging, Deena winks. "It's *how* he turned me down."

"How?" I sound a bit breathless. She's killing me here drawing this story out.

"He said, and I quote, 'Deena, babe, when we do it for the first time, it's gonna mean something.'"

I'm confused. "What did he mean by that? What did you say?"

Holding up her hand to stop the questions, she continues. "He told me he'd been waiting for me to cut his roommate loose for weeks. That I've been haunting his dreams." She covers her mouth and giggles. "His dreams. And that he's spent his nights thinking of all the things he wanted to do to me."

"Wow." I wonder what those things are? I should ask Lucky….

"Then he said, 'When we make love for the first time'"—she winks—"It's not going to be at your apartment after some random party. It's going to be somewhere special. I'm going to make sure it's everything you deserve, my queen.'"

"My queen?" I squeak. "I've always wanted someone to call me that." I have. Honest to goodness. I've read it in several books, and it always makes me swoon.

"That's right, bitch. I'm his queen."

"That's. So. Freaking. Awesome." And I mean every single one of those words. That's exactly what my best friend deserves. Finally, a guy who sees what a prize she is. Sure, she's annoying occasionally, but who isn't. She's genuine and sweet and generous, and above all else, she's loyal. I feel the burn of tears again. "I'm so happy for you."

She shrugs, but her smile hasn't left her face. "I've got a good feeling about him."

"Me too."

"I just hope he isn't doing this because he's got a micropenis or something."

And bam, the tears are gone. Replaced with gales of laughter.

And what the heck is a micropenis?

Before I can even ask the question, she's there with her phone in front of my face displaying a page full of very small man parts.

"That's not really a thing, is it?"

"Sadly. Yes."

"HAVE YOU EVER HEARD OF A MICROPENIS?"

Lucky's hand suddenly stops. It was previously moving up and down my bare hip and thigh. "Uh, why do you ask?"

"Keep doing that with your hand and I'll tell you."

There's no hesitation; he continues caressing me. *Caressing.* That's the exact right word for it too. "Deena's worried Theo's got one."

His hand stops again, causing a frown to cross my face. Reaching down, I place my hand on top of his and force it to move again. I guess he finds this funny, because he chuckles. "Are you asking me if I've seen his dick or something?"

"No." I blink. "Have you?"

"Babe." He rolls onto his back, and the sheet that's covering both of us slides down and stops right above his… *not* micropenis. "I'm not going to tell you about another guy's cock."

"Why not?" I push myself up until I'm sitting on his bed, holding the sheet up over my chest. Lucky reaches up and takes the edge of the sheet between two fingers and tugs. "Not until you answer my question."

"Why not what? Why am I not going to discuss another guy's dick with you?" He tugs again; this time he's successful. But I'm not bothered by it. I like that he wants to see me like this.

"Yes. All I want to know is does Theo Blazek have a micropenis or not?"

Lucky snorts. "Not that I am aware."

"Not that you're aware, or not that you'll admit to for sure one way or the other?"

"Foxy." Lucky growls. "If I tell you, you're going to have to make it up to me."

"Oh?" I arch my brow. "How, pray tell, am I to make it up to you?"

He pushes down the sheet, and I see Lucky's ready to go again. "You're going to swing one of those gorgeous legs over my hip so you can straddle me."

I swallow. "I'll try."

"Fine." He runs one hand through his hair. "He's got a normal dick."

"Big, like you?" I turn and reach for my phone that's sitting on the nightstand on my side of the bed.

Lucky growls. "What the fuck are you doing?"

"Texting Deena." I type out a quick message.

Me: Good news. Theo doesn't have a tiny penis. Yay!

"She's worried he's avoiding sex with her because of the penis thing." It's been a week since the party. She's been out with him twice. She even made him dinner at our place. Granted, she's not particularly skilled in the kitchen. Her idea of a home-cooked meal is the blue box of mac and cheese and hotdogs. I was just leaving the apartment as they sat down to eat, and from my perspective, he didn't seem to mind one bit.

"That's it." Lucky reaches out, grabbing my phone. When he gets it, he tosses it back onto the table and reaches for me. Placing his hands on my waist, he lifts me up. Off the bed.

"Lucky. No. You'll hurt your ribs." I place my hands on either side of his head and swing my left leg over him so I'm straddling him. I look down between us then up at him, not sure what to do next.

"Sit."

"Sit?" On him. *He wants me to sit. On him.* All this when I've still got questions. "So, is he big or small?"

"Not answering that, babe. You got the intel you needed. He doesn't have the microdick. Yeah?" He says that last part as he slides his fingers between my legs. I hear my phone chime but choose not to check for Deena's response. I'm sure it's something like "Phew!" or "Hell yes!" Either way, it doesn't require a response.

When he rubs my clit, I can no longer speak. So, I nod, and from that point on, I let Lucky take the lead.

And boy, can he lead.

35

———

EPILOGUE: BECKLYN

"Congratulations, beautiful."

I'm looking up at my boyfriend of, what is it now? Two and a half years. "Thanks, babe." He's holding a large bouquet of roses and giving me the biggest smile I've ever seen. You see, I graduated. Finally. I'm now a secondary science teacher.

An unemployed secondary science teacher, but that was by design. I've had several offers from districts around Urbana-Champagne, but I'm waiting to accept one until we know more about Lucky's job. He applied for something in Chicago, but the job he really wants is in Madison, Wisconsin. Which means, if he gets it, we'll be moving there, and I'll be doing some additional work so I'll be licensed to teach in that state as well.

"You look amazing today, girlfriend." That's Deena. Deena, who isn't graduating today. And maybe not ever.

It's not a surprise. She was never really into school. I think if she added up all of her credits, she'd be close to graduating, but she's more focused on her career as the girlfriend of an NFL quarterback. According to her, it's a full-time job.

"You look great too. Is Theo here?"

"Somewhere." She looks around the room but doesn't seem

209

too concerned. "He saw some of the guys from the team, so he's talking to them."

I wrap my arms around her. "Thanks for coming." They live in San Diego now. It's not just a quick drive to Illinois for them.

"No worries." She leans in. "Shh, don't tell, but Theo's talking to the Bears."

"Really?" I squeal. "Does that mean you might be living back here?"

"I hope so," she says, sounding exasperated. "I'm sick of all that sunshine."

"Ha, ha. Funny," I deadpan. "I miss you so much. I hope it works out."

"Me too." It's no joke. She's been gone over a year now, and I've missed her like crazy. Theo was drafted after his senior year and by then, they were a done deal. At least that's how Theo explained it. Somehow, he knew she was the one for him even while she was dating his roommate. Good thing for her, he was patient. About everything. He made her wait *six months* before doing the deed. Afterwards, she wouldn't tell me anything about their first time.

I take that back. She did say he definitely did *not* have a micropenis. By then, though, she was so far gone, I don't think it would've mattered if he had one or not.

"Hey, let's go. Your folks are waving us over." I take Lucky's hand and wave to Deena. "See you tonight?" I'm having a little party at Lucky's place to celebrate my graduation. Actually, we rented out the clubhouse for the event. I can't wait.

"Wouldn't miss it for the world."

36

EPILOGUE: LUCKY

"THIS IS IT." I SLAP JOE ON THE BACK. HARD.

"Ouch. Shit, dude. That hurt."

"Sorry." Not sorry. I still haven't paid him back for the broken rib, but why would I? His plan worked. I got the girl. "Nerves."

"She have any idea you're doing this?"

"None." I smirk. "I've been careful."

The two of us are hiding behind the door to the kitchen in the clubhouse. I've been waiting for Becklyn to finish up greeting her guests. Our guests. Hell, even my dad's here. I invited him, of course, but that has never meant anything before. I'm glad it did this time. It's good to see him, actually. I've missed the moody ass.

"Now. Go now." Joe practically pushes me through the swinging door. Once I'm out in the main room, I see she's turned and making her way toward her parents. He's right. Now's the time.

"Becklyn?" I call as soon as I'm close enough.

"Yeah?"

"Can I speak with you a moment?" God, I sound so formal.

"What's up? Are you okay? You look a little pale."

"No." I smile weakly. "I'm good." Taking her hand, I pull her closer to me. "I, uh, just need to say something."

"Okay." She reaches up and touches my cheek. "You're clammy." Leaning closer, she asks, "You need to use the restroom?"

A burst of laughter escapes me. "No, babe. I'm good."

"You sure?"

"I'm sure." I've never been surer of anything in my entire life. I decide I need to do it before she tells everyone I have a 'tummy ache' or something. Lowering down to one knee, I look up at her. I can tell she's confused, but only for a second. That's when she realizes what's happening. And when she does, her hands move up to cover the shock. Her eyes start to get glossy as well. "Oh, Lucky."

"Let me say this. Yeah?"

She nods, but her hands are still covering her mouth—hell, half her face.

"Once upon a time, there was a girl. She was beautiful and smart and a little bit of a pain in the ass."

She laughs, and I'm suddenly less nervous.

"One day, a semi-handsome guy spots her, but he doesn't think much of it because he's rather clueless."

"I think I know that guy," a woman mutters from somewhere in the room.

Others titter with laughter.

"Anyhoo…"

Becklyn lowers her hands and laughs louder. "You're such a dork."

"I know."

Reaching into my front pocket, I feel around for it. My mom's ring. When I called my dad to tell him I was going to propose to Becklyn, he told me he'd been holding on to Mom's ring. That she would have wanted me to have it to give to my future bride. To say it has meaning, well, that's a fucking understatement. And the fact my dad was willing to give it to me tells me that he's finally healing from her loss.

Pulling the ring out, I hold it up to her. "This was Mom's ring. My dad told me she'd want you to have it, and I believe him. I couldn't give this to anyone but you, Becklyn." Nobody else would be worthy.

"Lucky." Becklyn's crying now.

"Marry me?"

"Of course." She sniffles. "Of course I'll marry you. You're the man of my dreams. You're my best friend. I can't wait to marry you."

I stand up and wrap my arms around her, lifting her off her feet, and kiss her like it's our last kiss, when actually, it feels more like our first.

IF YOU ENJOYED LUCKY CHARMER, BE SURE TO CHECK OUT PICK-UP Lines Book 3: Double Dog Dare. Coming soon…

You may also enjoy the Palmer Sisters Series: *Meet the Palmer*

Sisters: six women, one man, their relationships with one another, and their crazy love lives. These books are short, sweet, and oh, so dirty.

Recently divorced, **Lainie Palmer-Bottoms** is a woman on a mission—a mission to jump-start her romance writing career with a sexy novel about a badass biker gang.

Keeton Gustafson is a badass biker dude and owner of Gustafson Custom Motorcycles. He's also Lainie Palmer-Bottoms's muse. The thing is, the second Keeton gets a look at the curvy beauty, it's him that's inspired.

At their first encounter, they discover they need each other. She needs research material for her novel. He needs to do her on his desk. Can two people from different worlds find common ground? Keeton thinks so, but Lainie's not so sure.

Thank you so much for reading! When I start a story, it begins with an outline, notes, and lots of crazy thoughts running through my head. When I actually start writing, the characters take over, leading me through the story like they're holding my hand--guiding me. The process is exciting and cathartic. With that said, I hope you enjoy the story.

If you did, please go to my website, www.kaytmiller.com, and join my newsletter so you can be the first to know what's coming up next. And…

And remember...Please, leave a review!

Thank you!

Chapter 1: Emma

"Do you generate electricity with water through the process of hydro power? Because dammmmm."

"Oh, god."

The memory of it… It's cringeworthy. No. It's more than that. It's… it's… humiliating.

Luckily, that guy doesn't know me from Adam. I'm 100% positive he's never seen me before and I really hope he never will again. I know this because there's no way a guy that looks like *that* and dresses in clothes that aren't standard issue college guy clothes is definitely not going to be seen on campus. No way.

No. I'm safe. Safe from having to face him again. Now, all I need to do it stop the scene from running on repeat through my brain. Oh, and I'll need to get my roommate and *former* best friend to stop laughing every time I walk into the kitchen.

She can be *so* annoying.

Flopping back onto my bed, I squeeze my eyes shut in an attempt to force myself to go to sleep. It's been almost two hours since I said those words--you know the ones above that pains me to repeat--and in that time, I've done everything in my power to make the memory of it go away.

Maybe if I start at the beginning, it'll exhaust me and I'll fall asleep...

Here goes.

Carley Dearborn, my closest and dearest friend, has been trying to pull me out of my shell for, well, all my life. We grew up in the same town and met when we went to the same elementary, middle, and high school together. We were practically connected at the hip. Even after graduation, when I told her where I wanted to go to college thanks to their excellent engineering department, she shrugged and said, "that sounded good to her". We lived in the dorms together our first year and then decided to move off campus the next.

To say we're tight is an understatement. I'd say she's the sister I never had. Okay, I've got a sister, but she and I don't get along but that's a story for another day.

So, as I said, Carley has been trying to yank me from my hard, turtle shell ever since we were kids and for the most part, she's been successful. I've tried things I never thought I would or could. Like swimming. I was terrified of the water but one day at the local pool, she took me by the hand and walked me into the water. She stayed with me in the baby pool until I was ready for more. That's the kind of friend she is. I should I say *was*. This thing tonight wasn't so gentle.

No, tonight was the "last straw". At least those were the words she used when she told me we were going out tonight. She didn't even warn me like she usually does. Ordinarily, she'd give me a few days to process the idea of doing something out of my comfort zone. But she didn't tonight. Instead, she stomped into my room after she got home from class, put her hands on her hips, and said, "Tonight. We're going out tonight and you're going to do it. You're going to approach a guy at the bar and you're going to talk to him."

The expression on her face sort of alarmed me. She looked scary. Angry. I had no idea where it was coming from since I hadn't recalled doing anything to make her that way. So, instead of arguing, I merely nodded. I mean, it was Friday night. Midterm exams were over. Sure, I had homework, but I always had homework and I could do that on Saturday and Sunday.

"Good." She said without a smile. "I'm going to choose your outfit and I'm doing your hair and makeup." She glared at me adding, "No arguments. Go take a shower."

Wow. Bossy. In her defense, I would've argued. It's my m.o. You know, modus operandi. It's cop show speak that means a particular way or method of doing something, especially one that is characteristic or well-established. Man, I love cop shows.

Anyway, I digress… I did as she instructed, er demanded, because I knew Carley wasn't in the mood for argument and I learned a long time ago when she got that way, it was just easier to go along. So, I shut my textbook on hydro-electric power, slid off my bed, and showered.

By the time we got to the bar, my stomach was doing flip flops. I mean, she had me in a *dress*. A dress! I never wear dresses especially not short ones. Sure, I've worn this one before *but with leggings*, for crying out loud. It's so short, if I bent over, you'd see my undies. In addition, she gave me big hair. I'm talking B-I-G hair. It's curly and wavy and it's got so much product in it, my fingers only get in about an inch before they get stuck.

And don't get me started on my makeup. The word trollop came to mind when I looked in the mirror, but that's an insult to trollops. "Sorry trollops." She gave me what she termed "smoky eyes" but what I'd refer to as vampire eyes all dark and suspicious looking. I look ridiculous. On top of that, my lips are red, *really* red. Luckily, most of the red ended up on the side of my first drink.

On top of all that. On top of the clothes and the hair and the makeup, she chose the swankiest joint in town for my humiliation. People don't even call it a bar. It's "a club". Believe me when I tell you, there's a difference. A bar is a place you go and have a beer. "A club" is fancy. There's a line out front to get in and according to my former bestie, you have to look a certain way to even get inside. Cue my current hideous ensemble.

The minute we stepped into the place; I did a complete one-eighty to leave The Dirty Rabbit. I don't know why they call it that because there's not a speck of dirt in the place unlike most of the campus bars we've been to. No, this place was *nice.* Which mean it's not our scene. It's not meant for college-aged people. A place like this is intended for professional people. People who don't have jobs, they have "careers".

The second I stepped into the place I froze. I was about to turn and march my big butt out of the place, Carley grabs my arm. "Where do you think you're going?"

Looking back and up at her, I gave her my best glare. "We can't afford this place. I bet drinks here are five bucks a piece."

"*I* invited *you* here, so I pay. You know the rule. Besides, we're not going to be here that long." She releases my arm and gives me a familiar look. I know what's coming. "You're going to have a drink for courage and then you're doing it." She shrugs then. "Besides. Dad sent me some money."

The eyeroll can't be held back, this time. "Of course, he did." Mr. Dearborn, better known as Daddy Moneybags, had an affair with is secretary when Carley was five and divorced Carley's mom soon after. Since then, she's seen him only a handful times even though he lives in Chicago—a mere hour from our hometown. When I say she's only seen him a handful of times, I'm not joking. Example. She saw him at her grandmother's funeral, at her high school graduation (he didn't stick around for the party after), and several times on accident, like the time at the Costco one town over from where we grew up. He was with a woman.

And not the one he had the affair with. A different one. One with several children in tow. To say that was awkward is an understatement.

No. Brad Dearborn is not present in her life, at all. Instead of spending quality time with his beautiful daughter, he sends her money as a parental substitute. Lots and lots of money. I know it hurts her. How could it not? The money comes in handy and she figures why not use it for good. Or in the case tonight, for evil.

Ordinarily, I would refuse to help her spend her dad's cash. It's not mine, after all. But tonight, I have no trouble helping her spend some of it and tonight because I'm going to need some liquid courage and I can't afford to fine establishments like this one.

As a matter of fact, until this week, I had no money coming in, but I finally landed a workstudy job at the library. (Thank goodness.) Because the word "broke" wasn't strong enough to describe my bank account. No, I'd say nearly destitute instead. And since my parents make just over minimum wage at a discount store in our hometown of Joliet, Illinois, a city about an hour southwest of Chicago, they sure aren't going to fund my night out. Don't get me wrong, my parents are awesome. Their kind and generous to a fault. They just don't have a pot to piss in, as they say. It's one of the reasons me and my sister don't get along, but I won't bore you with all that drama.

With no fight left in me, I follow Carley up to the bar where there are two open seats. Surprising because this place is packed with people, most of whom were wearing suits and work attire. I guess it makes sense for these people to go out on a Friday night after their work week. As Carley orders us our first drink, I take a moment to scan the bar. Most of the people here are young. I'd guess mid-twenties so that's good. At least we're not sticking out like a sore thumb here since we're both twenty-one. I feel something cool touch my fingers and look down at the drink Carley's placed next to my hand. I peek over at her. She's raised her glass and looking at me expectantly. "To new challenges."

I lift my drink which looks to be a vodka cranberry, my favorite, and tap my glass to hers. "To kicking your ass tomorrow for making me do this."

"Ha!" she laughs as she sips her drink. "Like you could kick my ass."

She's right. I'd never been able to do it. She's way bigger than me. Okay, not in the weight department. I'm pretty sure we weigh about the same. The difference is she's eight inches taller than me so the pounds we both carry are stretched out on her. Yeah, on her they look good. On me, not so much.

Actually, Carley is mostly my opposite in everything. Like I said, she's tall, I'm not. Her hair is blonde, while mine is more of a mousy brown hue. She's athletic having played most sports in high school while I was more of a mathlete. Still am. She's open, spontaneous, and funny. I'm closed off, nervous, and awkward. I guess that's why we've been friends for so long. Opposites attract. At least, it works for us.

Heck, even tonight I know she means well. I should be angry with her, but how can I be when all she wants to do is help me. She's the one that has had to listen to me whine and even cry sometimes about the fact I've never had a boyfriend. Hell, I've only been kissed once and that, again, was all thanks to her and a party in middle school. She got a game of spin-the-bottle going and well, that's it. I spun the bottle and it landed on Shawn McNamara. I could tell by his expression that I was the last person he wanted to kiss but he did it because the bottle told him he had to.

"So, let's get a couple of drinks in you and then we'll choose the guy."

I quickly downed the rest of my drink because, oh, god, she's *really* going to make me do it this time.

She's tried in the past but to no avail. Those times she even helped me prep. We talked about what I'd say once I stepped up to the guy. We rehearsed it, for goodness sake. But, every time I approached a guy, I'd freeze up, turn, and walk straight back to our table or out the door, whichever was closer. Honestly, I have no idea why she thinks tonight is going to be any different.

"And before you chicken out like you usually do, let me tell you why it's going to work tonight. Why I chose this place."

Holding up my glass, I make eye contact with the bartender. When he sees me, he quickly steps in front of us. "Need another one, beautiful?" Then he winks.

Oh, the urge to roll my eyes is almost too much to bear but I don't do it. I keep my eyes in place. "Yes."

"Be right back."

Turning to Carley, I wait for her to tell me why she chose the fanciest club in town.

"I chose this place because we don't know anyone here."

I look around just as the bartender returns with my drink. "That'll be ten-fifty."

I nearly choke at his words. "For a tiny drink?" I squeak. Carley's right about one thing, you won't find college students at a bar like this one because no college student could afford this place.

Carley hands over her credit card which gets her a wink from the bartender.

Once he's gone, she continues. "And because we won't know anyone here, you can approach a guy––a guy that you'll never see again."

"Okay." I nod as I take a long pull from my drink. "I can see the benefits of that." I really can.

"So, because of that, I say you should choose the hottest guy in the place." She shrugs. "I mean, why not?"

Why not? I can tell her about a million reasons why not, but I don't. "I guess."

"I'm thinking *that* guy." I follow her line of sight until it lands on a guy that belongs on the cover of a magazine.

"Him?" I practically choke on the last little bit of my drink. Because *that* guy is way out of my league. From here, I can tell he's tall. Plus, he looks built like he's got some muscle beneath that suit jacket. That's not the best part of him, though. It's his face… is perfect. Like a young Paul Newman.

Now, before you think that's an odd comparison, my mom loves Paul Newman. She has every single one of his movies on VHS and if you were to look him up: young Paul Newman, you'd agree that the man was gorgeous. This guy has the same sort of wavy, golden brown hair. I can't see his eye color from here but part of me hopes they're the same blue as Newman's.

Ugh. Why am I going off on a tangent about Paul Newman?

Because thinking about something else is calming.

Not to mention his salad dressing is pretty good. And he, well, he's no long with us, but his company still gives away much of their profits to important organizations. And I do my best to support companies who are trying to do good in this world. Especially companies who are working to help our environment. I know this because it's one of the reasons I chose my major in alternative energy. The earth needs our help.

"Hello?" Carley is waving her hand in front of my face. "Yoo hoo. Earth to Emma."

She makes me laugh. "Sorry."

"Off on one of your brain tangents again?"

That's what she calls it when I space off. "Yeah. This one was about Paul Newman."

Carley looks over toward the guy. "Ooh, he does look like a young Paul Newman. In that movie…" she snaps her fingers together like she's trying to remember the name.

I say, "The Long, Hot Summer."

"Yessss." Carley slaps my arm. "That one." She glances at the guy again. "Definitely. Newman was sexy as fuck in that one."

"He was." I nod all while trying to think of something else to distract my friend because my thought is if I get her drunk and talking, she'll forget all about me doing this-this stupid, embarrassing, and self-destructive act.

Yeah. Yeah. I know. It's not *that* bad.

"Right." She drinks the last of her cocktail, claps her hands together, and says, "Right. Let's do this."

Crap.

"Paul Newman is the one." She nods in his direction.

"Yeah." She smiles brightly. "He's gorgeous." And he's not alone. He's with a group. Of about six or seven other guys. All of whom are very good looking. They're more Carley's kind of guys. At least, they're the kind of guys who like her. She's like a bee to honey to that kind of man. If that makes any sense.

Funny, though. She doesn't seem all that interested in guys right now. It doesn't stop them, though.

"You know what?" I turn to face her again. "*You* should talk to him. He seems more your type."

"Nope..." She shakes her head slowly and I can't help but notice that her hair moves when she does. Unlike mine which is more like a helmet. It's armor, I guess, which is a good thing. I need battle-ready gear. "...my sweet Emma, this is about you."

I hate when it's about me.

"I don't think I can do it." I mean, he's not alone. Those other guys... "If he were alone."

"Well, let's have another drink and we'll wait until he approaches the bar or something."

"I'm gonna need a shot." I mumble under my breath, but she hears.

Raising her hand to the bartender, he steps over. "Another?" he asks with a smile and another wink. My god, the guy is shameless. Plus, you'd think his eye would stick like that the number of times he winks a night.

"Two shots of tequila, please."

"Not tequila." I moan. She knows what tequila does to me. It makes me brave.

Winky is back before I can argue.

"You need it. Now shut up and drink."

"Fine." I throw back the golden liquid and wince as it burns down my throat. "I hate you." I hiss.

"I heard that." She takes her shot. "And no you don't." Looking over in his direction, Carley raises her hands so they're right below her chin and claps. "Ooh, he's on the move," she says excitedly.

I turn my head in time to see the target of tonight's humiliation approach the bar. Except, he's not alone. Two of the guys from his group are with him. "He's not alone." I whine.

"Go." She practically pushes me off my stool. "Get 'er done."

"I can't."

"You *can* and you will."

I shake my head. I wish I could tell you my hair went with me, but I can't.

"Go."

I take a moment to look at the guy I'm supposed to talk to. He's so… everything. "He's not the right one." I say as a droplet of sweat starts to run down my forehead. "He's too pretty."

"No. He's just a guy. He probably lives with his mommy."

I suddenly laugh. Because that was funny. Turning to Carley, I look her in the eye. "You know dang well that he," I point in his general direction, "doesn't live with mommy." No, a guy like that… he's got his own house. Maybe a condo. A nice one.

I wait for her to tell me we can leave but that's not what I get. "You're really going to make me do it, aren't you?"

I glance at the man then back to Carley. "Do what?" I don't know what she's talking about.

"Fine. But just remember you made me do this." She sighs. "I double dog dare you."

I'm suddenly frozen. I can't breathe. Or blink. *"What?"* The word comes out as a screech.

"You heard me." She's starting to sound like the angry Carley from earlier. The one that stood in my bedroom doorway and commanded I go out tonight.

"Really?" That time I sounded squeaky.

"Really. I've coddled you for far too long. I'm proclaiming this a double dog dare situation."

A double dog dare situation?

"You're invoking the triple D? *For this?*" I have to concentrate on my air intake because I'm seriously shocked. "It's not *that* bad?" I mean, seriously? We hold the D.D.D. with high esteem. It's so revered, we've never actually used it.

"Yes, it's *that* bad. I've been trying to get you to talk to a guy for two and a half years. You're a junior now. You're going to graduate in a year and eight months. What kind of best friend would I be if you left here without talking to a stupid guy?"

"I talk to guys."

"Those nerds in your engineering classes don't count."

"Hey." I'm about to defend those nerds in my engineering classes when she holds up her hand.

Excuse me? *She's giving me her hand?*

"They're nerds. Just like you."

"Hey!" This time I have to defend myself, at least.

"There's nothing wrong with being a nerd. You're going to make three times more than me when we go out into the work-force. So, I don't feel sorry for you. But we can hash that stuff out tomorrow. Right now." She places her hand on my shoulder. "Right now, you're going to march your little tushy over to that hotty and you're going to talk to him." She gives me a warm smile then she does it again. She pulls out the big guns. "I double dog…"

"I *know.*" I say it so loudly, the people around us can hear so, I repeat it quietly, "I know. You double dog dared me." Which means, I have to do it this time. *I have to*. It's the promise we made to each other in ninth grade. If we double dog dared the other, we *had* to do it. It is rare, sacred, and once uttered, unbreakable.

The only good thing about getting this over with.... The sooner I do, the sooner we can leave and the sooner I can go home, change into my comfy clothes, and eat my weight in some kind of cookie which *she's* doing to buy now that she's forcing my hand. It's the least she can do.

Sliding off the stool, I push my dress down as far as it will go which isn't very dang far. I reach up and attempt to do something with my hair but it's not going anywhere. Taking in a lung full of air, I release it slowly.

"Quit dicking around and go." Carley's voice turned all growly on me. I don't like ti.

"Fine," I grit my teeth and growl. She's starting to irk me.

Taking a step, then another, and another, I make my way around the corner of the bar and spot him waiting in line to order. He's easily the tallest one by several inches. Not even his buddies are as tall. I take another step but this one feels like my feet are in quicksand. The closer I get, the harder it is to walk. And to breathe. My heart's pounding in my chest so hard it feels like it's gonna jump right out.

I flinch when someone speaks into my ear. Carley. "I know you're freaking out right now, but *you can do this*. Remember, you'll never see him again."

I nod because I can't speak.

"Ask him what his sign is."

His sign? She's talking about his Zodiac sign. I'm into that. Well, we're into that. Both Carley and I read our horoscopes every day and wait one gosh-dang minute. Turning to face her, I ask, "Did you read my horoscope today?"

Carley smirks. "Of course."

Now it all makes perfect sense. The reason she's dragging me out here today. The urgency of is because my stupid horoscope said something about romance and taking risks. "Carley…" I practically growl her name.

"What?" She looks a little surprised by my reaction. "This is meant to be. The stars say so. Now go." She touches my shoulder and gives me a gentle shove. "*Go*. And if you don't want to ask him his sign, use one of those pickup lines you read about."

Oh, right. One of the other times she's tried this, I prepared by looking up cute things to say when you first meet someone. I pause for a moment to think. Sure, some of them were pretty raunchy but there were a few I really liked. I even wrote one of my own. One that fits me perfectly. "Right." I nod and take a more self-assured step toward the man. The closer I get to him, the more I realize he is a *man*. He's definitely not a boy like so many of the guys, the nerds, I take classes with.

When I'm less than a foot away from him, I look down at his feet. He's wearing dress shoes. Nice ones. I can also see from here that his pants are black, the same color as his dress shirt. Taking a small step closer, I lean in, close my eyes, and take a whiff.

Yes, I realize that was probably weird to smell him, but I had to know.

Answer? He smelled good. *Very* good. Like musk and spice.

Before I could lose my nerve, I reached up and, with my pointer finger, I tapped him on the shoulder. I watch, like in slow motion, as he turns his head but he's looking above me. So I do what I can to draw his eyes down. I raise my hand and wave in front of his face. It worked. His head tilts down until our eyes meet.

Holy shite. He's got blue eyes. Probably not as blue as Paul's but pretty dang blue. I'd categorize them as steel blue. Sort of like his expressing which I'd refer to as his steely gaze. I'd also like to know that he's better looking up close than he was far away which is saying something because he was flipping gorgeous from across the room.

Oh, crud. I can't do this.

It's too much.

I glance back at Carley. She's leaning against the bar. Her left elbow is resting on the bar, her right hand is on her hip and her expression? If I told her her brow was arched so high it's nearly at her hair line, would you believe me? Plus, she's not smiling.

This is it. I have to do it. "No excuses this time, Emma."

"Huh?" The guy speaks. He actually speaks. It's too bad I don't have time to explain because I do it. With bravery I didn't know I had; I say what I need to say. "Do you generate electricity with water through the process of hydro power? Because *dammmmm.*"

I did it.

I said it.

I can't believe it.

Except… Time froze. It stood still as he stared at me. As he did, he blinked. I had no idea what to do next. I mean, I had no plan after I said what I said. I guess I assumed he'd chuckle, look at me adoringly, then he'd hug me or something.

That's not what happened.

Instead of the hug I so desperately needed, he blinked some more then said, "Uh… what?"

Ordinarily, when someone asks me a question, I answer it. Correctly. In this case, his 'What?' is asking me to repeat my previous statement which I'm hesitant to do.

"Huh?" I give him a few blinks of my own. When his eyes meet mine, I'm struck rather dumb. And believe me when I tell you, I'm *not* stupid.

"What did you say to me?" he asks again.

Wow, he's got a nice voice too. The man is the entire package.

Instead of doing what I should--you know… run--I repeat it. My personalized pick-up line. "I *said,* 'Do you generate electricity with water through the process of hydro power? Because dam'." This time I don't emphasize the last word because now that I've repeated it, it sounds really stupid. The two guys standing with him must agree because they're laughing.

Great.

Not only that, but the guy I just said those words to is smiling. Rather smugly, if I were being honest. I watch as the smug smirk on his face morphs into a toothy smile. It's like he's about to laugh at me too.

I'm right. It does change into a laugh. A chuckle, I guess is how I'd describe it. No matter. It's mortifying. Suddenly, he's not so good looking anymore.

Not in the least.

ACKNOWLEDGMENTS

Thank you to Hot Tree Editing for editing this book from start to finish.

And an extra special thank you to Becky at Hot Tree Promotions for your advice, expertise, and your positivity.

And for my beta readers.
Thank you so much for your time and feedback!

ABOUT THE AUTHOR

Kayt grew up in the midwest surrounded by a loving family which included three brothers, one sister, and parents who always fostered her creative side.

Kayt wrote her first book when she couldn't find a story about a certain type of a woman and a specific kind of man. She called it *Game Changer* and it couldn't have been a more appropriate title. It changed her life in many ways.

Her goal, as a writer, is to write stories that relate to all of us, to make readers laugh and maybe cry sometimes. Kayt hopes her readers can escape into a fantasy, one that's actually possible. Sure, some of the stories are dubbed "Insta-love" but that's okay. She fell in love with her husband pretty damn fast and with her daughter the second she saw her. So, it's a thing, she swears.

facebook.com/authorkaytmiller
twitter.com/kaytmiller1
instagram.com/kaytmiller1
bookbub.com/profile/kayt-miller